THE ARCHERS
RETURN TO AMBRIDGE

THE ARCHERS

RETURN TO AMBRIDGE

Jock Gallagher

BBC BOOKS

Published by BBC Books
A division of BBC Enterprises Ltd
Woodlands, 80 Wood Lane, London W12 OTT

First published 1988
© Jock Gallagher 1988

ISBN 0 563 20606 3

Set in 10/11 Times Roman by Opus, Oxford
and printed in Great Britain by
Richard Clay Ltd, Bungay, Suffolk

CHAPTER ONE

For Jack Archer the war was over. Not that it had ever really started as far as he was concerned. After three years of being pushed around a miserable barracks in Aldershot, the army had finally decided it didn't need him. Now he'd been discharged – "honourably" it said on his papers – but he knew differently. There could be no honour in walking away from a war.

Like most of his mates, Jack Archer had signed on as soon as he could because he wanted to be a hero. He wanted to do his bit for the country . . . to show Hitler what the British were made of . . . to kill a few Germans . . . to win the war!

At the time, the army had seemed to share his enthusiasm. The recruiting sergeant in Borchester had been keen to take him. Within days of his eighteenth birthday and fresh off his father's farm, he was on his way to the Borsetshires' regimental headquarters. He felt he was destined for greatness. There were medals to be won ... and some of them surely had Jack Archer's name on them.

It was a young doctor, only a couple of years older than he was, who had been the one to throw a spanner in the works. After carrying out a few peremptory tests and listening to Jack's slightly wheezy chest for a couple of seconds with a stethoscope, the MO had scribbled the cruel words . . . "unfit for active service" on his medical record. And that, Jack reflected, was the day the war really ended for him.

Whoever had said "They also serve who only stand and wait" had been wrong. Ask anyone who had done his time in the quartermaster's stores issuing boots to other lads so that they could march off to war and glory. Jack had never felt anything but useless in the service depot they'd sent him to. He had wanted to walk tall with his Borsetshire mates in the county regiment; he just could not adjust to life as a private in the Royal Army Service Corps. He had hated it. Yet he knew he should have been grateful not to have been in the thick of the fighting.

Stuck in the depot handing out equipment, he saw squads of new boys, dreamers with the gleam in their eye he had once had in his, going off to war. Thinking only of victory over the enemy, they were cheerful and noisy as they acquired the paraphernalia of killing. To them, the King's uniform was a magic cloak that would protect them from harm . . . and because they were right and the Germans were wrong, God was on their side.

And he had seen blokes his own age come back shattered in body and spirit . . . broken men who told terrible stories of carnage . . . of guns and shells and tanks and the noise and stench of war. They all spoke in the same monotonous voice . . . not complaining, just explaining. He could see the nightmare in their eyes as he relieved them of their battle-stained uniforms that had given no protection at all against the experiences they had just been through.

For Jack, the only saving grace of his time in the army was that he'd found himself a wife. Lance-corporal Peggy Perkins of the ATS, the clerk in charge of the stores, was a pretty, bright-eyed Londoner whose sharp Cockney wit had done much to relieve the gloom of Jack's surroundings. A smile from her had most of the men eating out of her hand. Life, said Peggy, was for living and if she had to do it in the shadow of war, she would simply have to make the best of a bad job.

She'd been gentle and kind with the war-shattered lads, listening patiently to their tales and holding their hands in the hope that she could help them to forget at least for a few moments. She'd been friendly and cheerful with the rest without leading them on. She'd fended off their passes with a good nature and her banter had left even the most ardent of them chuckling in their frustration!

It had taken Jack, a shy young man from a rural backwater, a long time to pluck up the courage to ask Peggy for a date. He'd been out with several of the village girls (one in particular, Elsie Catcher, he'd fancied quite a bit, he remembered) but although they'd all been pretty enough, none of them had been half as bright and attractive as Peggy Perkins. It had taken him even longer to ask her to marry him and Jack still couldn't quite believe she'd said "yes".

But there was no doubting the evidence of his own eyes. There she was on the seat opposite him, eight months pregnant with his baby and sleeping fitfully as the train hurtled through the darkness of the English winter. The army, having no further use for him, had given him his discharge, and now he was taking his new wife back to Ambridge, his home village, to meet his family for the first time.

Looking around in dissatisfaction, he tried to brush the grime of the compartment off his uniform. Third class wasn't the way he'd wanted to bring his wife home but on the miserable wage he'd earned as a buckshee private, he couldn't stretch to anything better. All his discharge money had gone on buying a few extra civvy clothes to go with his demob suit. That was carefully folded in his kit-bag in the overhead rack. Since no one had asked him to hand back his army gear he'd kept it; he'd always been determined to make his return home in uniform . . . even if it wasn't that of the famous Borsetshires. Anyway, it would be useful later for working in around the farm.

Peggy had stayed on in the ATS after they'd been married, but as soon as she discovered she was pregnant, she had been given her discharge too and the little money she'd saved up she'd spent mainly on a layette for the baby. After the long journey, the one maternity dress she'd been able to buy for herself looked as badly creased as his khaki.

Jack felt a twinge of remorse, remembering he'd spent his last few shillings on a tot of whisky and a glass of beer when they'd changed trains at Reading. He'd thought it might deaden the boredom of the long, tiresome journey ahead. He was wrong. It had only made him feel even more miserable and the constant click of the train's wheels on the lines as they roared and rattled along through the late evening darkness, almost matched the throbbing in his head.

Jack looked anxiously at Peggy as she groaned softly to herself. Heavily pregnant as she was, she must be finding it almost impossible to get comfortable on the hard, narrow seat as the train rocked from side to side. She wasn't the complaining type, though, and true to form she was simply making the best of it.

They seemed to have been travelling for ever on crowded trains with squealing kids and noisy servicemen sprawling all over the place. It was only after they'd changed at Moreton Morrell for the last leg of the wearying journey that Jack had managed to wangle a compartment to themselves and Peggy had managed to stretch out a bit. He peered out of the fogged-up window into the darkness outside, hoping to recognise a familiar landmark, but he couldn't see a thing through the steam and condensation. Still, it couldn't be long before they arrived at Hollerton Junction, the nearest station for Ambridge.

Jack wasn't quite sure what to expect when they got there. He'd written asking his father to meet them at the station, but as usual he'd left it to the last minute to post the letter so he couldn't even be sure it had got to Brookfield Farm yet!

Once again he wondered what the future held for him and Peg. He hoped she'd fit into village life after the hustle and bustle of the city. He couldn't help worrying that her view of the country owed a bit too much to chocolate-box images of pretty little cottages with roses round the door and a few chickens pecking in the run at the bottom of the garden. Did she realise, he wondered, how much hard work it took just to stand still on a farm?

8

Jack was taking it for granted that he'd have a job waiting for him at Brookfield as he had before going into the army. He assumed that his parents would be able to put them up until they'd found a cottage of their own. He'd gathered from his mother's letters, and his father's scribbled notes at the bottom, that young Phil, his kid brother, was doing a few things around the place now, but he was only a slip of a lad and couldn't be much of a substitute for proper help. His father would welcome some real help around the farm. Some of the glumness eased away and Jack almost smiled. It would be nice to be back in his home surroundings.

He looked at his watch, a present from his mother when he'd joined up, and guessed they'd be pulling into the station in about five or ten minutes. He gently shook his wife awake.

"Come on, Peg, old girl. It's not far now to the promised land. It's nearly time to meet the Archer family!"

Peggy opened her eyes and blinked in the dim light.

"Are we nearly there, Jack?"

"Aye, we are. How are you feeling?"

She eased herself upright and tried unsuccessfully to smooth down her wrinkled dress.

"I feel as if I've been drawn through one of your perishing hedgerows backwards . . . but I'll live!"

Jack grinned at her. Born and brought up in the East End of London, she might never have been in the countryside before, but she'd been doing plenty of mugging up beforehand and now she kept dropping what she thought were appropriate expressions into her conversation.

"They're not just my hedgerows any more, Peg. They're ours now! We're going home, girl. My folks will soon have you as right as rain."

She smiled back nervously.

"I don't 'arf hope they'll take to me. D'you fink they'll mind my accent?"

"Wot accent's that then, mate?"

Jack couldn't resist teasing her. She had several spots of soot on her face and her dishevelled hair made her look very vulnerable. She stuck out her tongue at him . . . a reminder that she was still only nineteen.

"Come to fink about it, your own country-bumpkin accent ain't all that 'ot, is it?"

Peggy's accent was a moveable feast. Sometimes you could hardly have placed her as coming from London; at other times, such as now, you could tell her mum must have been deafened by the sound of Bow Bells while she was being born. Before Jack could think of a suitably scathing response, the brakes went on with a great grinding noise and they lurched into each other as the train suddenly slowed down. Jack put his arms protectively round his wife.

"Don't you worry, Peg. Mum and Dad will love you nearly as much as I do . . . Cockney accent and all! And I'm sure you'll love them too."

As the train finally juddered to a halt. He looked out to see the station name and then remembered that all the signs had been removed to confuse the Germans if they ever managed to invade. Despite the black-out, he was just able to recognise the familiar station.

"Here we are, Peg. Hollerton Junction . . . no mistaking that!"

He helped her onto the platform through a great cloud of steam hissing from a pipe under the train. The platform lights were too dim for him to tell if his father was one of the little knot of people waiting at the ticket barrier. He swung his kit-bag over his shoulder, picked up Peggy's battered suitcase and led the way towards the exit.

His father wasn't there.

Jack watched with a feeling of growing panic mixed with annoyance as the people waiting greeted their relatives and friends and disappeared off into the night. He looked around. There was no sign of his father's car and – even worse – there wasn't a taxi on the rank.

It wouldn't have mattered if there had been. To his horror, he realised they didn't have enough money for the journey to Ambridge – it had all gone on that blasted drink at Reading.

"Hell, Peg, I don't understand it! My letter must have gone astray. Dad would have been here for sure if he'd had it. He wouldn't let us down."

Peggy shrugged her shoulders. She was used to Jack's lack of organisation. She'd spent most of her time in the ATS sorting things out after Jack and the other men were supposed to have arranged them.

"Never mind, we'll just have to walk."

"Walk? We can't walk to Ambridge in the pitch dark. It's more than two and a half miles. It would take us half the night. Anyway, you wouldn't get very far in your condition."

Peggy shivered.

"Well, even so, anything's better than hanging around here. It's perishing cold. If we don't move pretty sharpish, we'll freeze to death. Can't we at least go into the waiting-room until we've thought what to do?"

Jack put his arm round her. Her thin coat wasn't much help in keeping out the sharp wind whistling around the bleak station.

"I'm sorry, Peg . . ."

"Don't keep saying you're sorry, Jack. I know you are, and I'm sorry too, but it's not your fault."

"Yes it is. I should have written to Dad earlier."

"Of course you should have done, but blaming yourself won't do no good now. Let's get into the warm and sort ourselves out."

The clip-clop of a pony and trap interrupted their conversation. For a second, Jack thought it might be his father and started hurrying towards it. No such luck. It was a young lad who sat on the narrow driving seat. Disappointed, Jack turned back towards the waiting-room.

"Jack!"

The boy called his name again.

"Jack! It's me . . . Phil!"

Jack turned to gaze at him in astonishment and relief.

"Look, Peg. I told you Dad wouldn't let us down. He's sent our Phil to meet us. It's young Phil. I wouldn't have recognised him."

It was more than a year since the two brothers had last seen each other. Philip had been at school still, and at that awkward, gawky age when he'd looked as if a good puff of wind would have knocked him over. Jack stared at him now as he climbed down from the trap.

"Well, lad, you might not have grown up much, but you've certainly grown out."

The younger brother was no longer a skinny kid. Shorter than Jack, his shoulders had broadened out and he looked as strong as an ox. His heavy overcoat emphasised his bulk.

"Dad's very sorry he couldn't be here to meet you in the car but we've got a problem with one of the animals and he couldn't leave it. I'm not allowed to drive yet so you'll have to make do with this thing, I'm afraid. It's a bit draughty and Prince isn't too nippy on his feet any more but it's better than walking!"

He suddenly remembered his manners.

"Oh . . . is this your wife?"

Jack gave a short laugh.

"Of course it's my wife. Who else do you think it is? The Queen of Sheba? Peg . . . this is my kid brother, Philip!"

"Pleased to meet you, Philip. It's ever so kind of you to come all this way on a freezing cold night to meet us."

Jack noticed his wife had carefully ironed out most of her Cockney accent. He was slightly cross. For some reason he couldn't have explained, he didn't want her putting on airs and graces in front of his family, but he decided to let it pass without comment in front of his younger brother.

12

He heaved the kit-bag and case into the trap.

"Let's get you on board now. Easy as you go, Peg. It's quite a stretch."

Philip had brought two heavy blankets with him and Jack wrapped one round Peggy's shoulders and tucked the other one round her legs. She smiled at him gratefully.

"I feel as snug as a bug in a rug, now."

"Right then Phil . . . home . . . and don't spare the pony!"

Philip flicked the long driver's whip at the pony's ears and as it trotted smartly out of the station yard, Jack Archer looked at his wife. She didn't seem to mind the unexpected mode of transport . . . probably thought it was the normal thing for this backward part of rural England. But now that the immediate crisis was over, he felt quite angry. Surely, just this once, his father might have put him first. There must have been someone else who could have coped with the blasted sick animal. Jack hadn't exactly been expecting a hero's welcome, but it was a pretty poor show to be met by his kid brother . . . and by his kid brother in a wretched horse and cart! That was no kind of welcome at all.

He'd been brought up on his mother's stories of how Uncle Ben had returned from the Great War in 1918 with the village band waiting for him and everyone lining the road cheering and shouting. She'd been in service then, but she'd been given the afternoon off to join in the celebrations which had lasted as long as there was ale in the barrel and enough men still standing to drink it.

That, Jack thought, was how a soldier should return from the war . . . walking tall and proud with the sun glinting on his brass buttons. Instead, he was slinking back into Ambridge at the dead of night. Folk would probably have forgotten he'd ever been away!

He tried to recall the rest of the story about his uncle's homecoming but he found it difficult to sort the myth out from the reality. He did know, though, that his father Dan and his younger brother Ben had both worked at Brookfield Farm for their father before going into the army. Ben had been in the thick of the action in Belgium and France when Grandfather Archer had died, but his father was still at the regimental depot waiting to be sent to the front. Instead he'd been given a compassionate discharge to return home to run the farm.

When Ben eventually returned at the end of the war, things hadn't worked out well between the brothers and there'd been some sort of row which ended in Uncle Ben going off to live in Canada. Rumour had it that part of the trouble was because they were both in love with the same girl. Jack couldn't be sure about that but he knew that it was his father who'd married Doris Forrest, and had stayed on to make a success of Brookfield Farm.

Jack glanced at his younger brother and then at his wife squeezed up close beside him, and half asleep again. At least if there was going to be any conflict between him and young Phil, it could only be over the farm!

The journey from Hollerton Junction to Ambridge took the best part of forty minutes and by the time the horse and trap turned into the yard, all three of them were cold and exhausted.

Doris Archer rushed outside to greet them as they clambered stiffly out of the trap. A small, slightly plump woman with greying hair cut short and pressed into two waves at the side of her head, she didn't look the sort that two men would have fought over. Her face wore a great beaming smile as she threw her arms round her eldest son.

"Oh, Jack. It's lovely to have you home."

Then she turned quickly to Peggy, who was looking slightly lost in the strange surroundings.

"And this is your new wife? Hello, Peggy."

As she hugged her, she noticed the young girl's cheek was icy cold.

"Oh, whatever am I thinking of, keeping you out here like this? Come into the house quickly before you freeze to death."

"Thank you, Mrs Archer. I do have to confess as to how it is a bit nippy."

Everyone laughed at her understatement, and again Jack noticed that the Cockney accent had been disguised. He would have to watch that.

Inside, Peggy looked around the big kitchen in awe. It was spotlessly clean and there was a huge fire roaring in the range. On the big square table was a magnificent spread of cold meats, bread, cheese, pickles and lots of other things in pots and bottles and jars. It was exactly what she'd imagined a farm kitchen would look like.

"Oh, Mrs Archer, it's perfect. It's just the picture Jack painted for me. There's not a thing out of place!"

Doris Archer appreciated the compliment.

"Thank you, Peggy . . . but I think I'd prefer it if you called me Doris . . . or Mum if you'd rather . . ."

Halfway through the sentence, she suddenly noticed Peggy's condition and let out a squeal of delight.

"You're expecting a baby!"

Jack hadn't thought to mention it in his letters.

"When's it due?"

Peggy wasn't sure whether or not to be annoyed by Jack's failure to tell his family about the baby. She'd work that out later.

"In about a month."

"Good heavens . . . come and sit down at once. You must be half dead with all that travelling."

After fussing and making sure Peggy was comfortable, she turned to Jack.

"You're a bright one, my lad. Whyever didn't you tell us Peggy was expecting? We'd have come and fetched you from Aldershot. We wouldn't have let you travel all that way by train and we'd certainly not have let you bring her home in that old bone-shaker of a trap. Whatever were you thinking of? Whatever must poor Peg think of her new in-laws?"

15

Jack didn't know what to say.

"I'm sorry, Mum. You know I'm not very good at letter-writing."

He knew it sounded pathetic. Doris Archer was not impressed.

"That's no excuse. You're about to become a father and your dad and I about to become grandparents and you never let on. Is that all you think of us? Didn't you think we had a right to know? Didn't you think we would want to help?"

Just then the door opened and Dan Archer came in. Although he'd been out working in the barn, he was in his shirt sleeves. He didn't appear the slightest bit bothered by the cold. It just didn't seem to affect him.

He was only a couple of inches taller than his son but he was very much broader with a deep barrel chest and powerful arms. To Peggy, he looked every inch the English farmer. His weatherbeaten face beamed.

"Ah . . . the return of the prodigal. Hello Jack . . . how are you lad?"

"I'm fine, Dad."

There was an awkward pause as the two contemplated how to greet each other. The older man allowed his natural reserve to drop first. He put his arms round his son.

"You look fine, Jack. It's grand to have you home again! Now let's have a look at this new wife you've brought with you . . ."

He, too, stopped in surprise when he saw Peggy.

"But you're . . ."

Doris came to the rescue.

"Aye, Dan. We're to be grandparents you and I . . . fancy that!"

Peggy enjoyed all the fuss and attention and it stopped her being cross with Jack for not having mentioned the baby.

If she was honest, she had to admit she was so much in love with Jack that she didn't mind any of his faults. Given a bit more time she'd straighten out any little wrinkles. Now she was delighted to be welcomed into the bosom of his family. She was a long way from London, but she had a feeling that if Dan and Doris Archer had anything to do with it, she was going to enjoy life in the heart of England.

CHAPTER TWO

Great snowflakes fluttered and swirled around Jack as he walked up Lakey Hill. He filled his lungs with the cold air, but there was no sign of the wheeze that had worried the army doctor so much. He took another deep breath. It was a great feeling. He was home. No more queues of squaddies waiting to be kitted out . . . no more endless bits of paper to fill out . . . no more angry sergeants to bawl him out.

Down below, Ambridge lay half-hidden under a snug blanket of snow. It was a glorious sight, prettier than any Christmas card. He felt at peace. The war was a long way away. This lonely English hillside was probably the most peaceful place on earth, he thought.

He and Peggy had been back at Brookfield for little more than a fortnight and already the grim shadows of army life were beginning to lift. Peg seemed to have taken to farm life so well it was hard to believe she hadn't been born and brought up in Ambridge alongside him. Their time in the Aldershot stores seemed only a dim interlude to be put behind them.

It wasn't quite as easy as that, of course. He still had sleepless nights thinking about some of the friends he had seen go off to France, young men who'd known nothing of the world, who'd never been beyond their home-town or village before they joined the army. Some had never known love or held a woman in their arms. Others had never tasted milk warm from the cow or walked in the open fields. For too many of them, all thought and feeling had ended in pain and fear in the desert warfare of North Africa or on the battle-scarred beaches of Normandy.

Sometimes, late at night, Jack wondered if he would ever forget. Would he ever stop feeling guilty that he had stayed behind? Would he ever stop wondering if he would have been a hero when the crunch had come and he'd had to face up to the enemy?

In the daylight, and especially on days like today when he could wander freely along the paths he'd discovered as a boy and breathe in God's good, clean air he felt there might be hope. Every time he heard Peggy laughing, every time he thought about the expected baby – would it be a boy or a girl? – he knew he was easing further away from the abyss of despair into which he might so easily have tumbled without her. Tomorrow, he knew, was much more important than yesterday.

Jack would have liked to have been better prepared for the arrival of his first child. Perhaps if he hadn't wasted three years of his life counting out bootlaces and gas-masks he would have been in a better position to support them. Perhaps if they'd waited for another year or so before they'd got married, he'd have been able to put a few bob together. Perhaps if he'd stayed at home, on the grounds of farming being a reserved occupation, he'd have been closer to having a farm of his own.

That's really what he wanted . . . to stride across a few acres that he could call his own, to decide for himself whether or not to grow barley or potatoes, whether to concentrate on building up a dairy herd or to settle for sheep. Perhaps it would happen? One day, perhaps? Perhaps . . . perhaps was a word too often in his thoughts.

Up on Lakey Hill, Jack's fantasies could take flight and reach all the way out to New Zealand where his Uncle Frank was said to have thousands of acres of prime sheep-grazing land and to run more than twenty different flocks. One day, Jack told himself, he would do the same. Here in England, Jack Archer would be as grand a farmer as Frank Archer was today on the far side of the world. Dreams cost nothing up there on Lakey Hill. It was only a question of making up his mind about the direction he wanted to go. Up on Lakey Hill, he was king.

The wind was rising now, blowing the swirling snow into his face, making it quite difficult to see anything. He decided he'd better get back to Brookfield Farm – it was nearly mid-day and Peggy and his mother would be competing to see who could prepare the most mouth-watering meal. Although Doris would have been more than happy to cook for them all, Peggy had insisted from the start that she should look after herself and Jack.

He smiled again. He'd married a real battler. Despite her fast-expanding figure, she bustled around the kitchen, cooking and cleaning. She even tried to help out with the chickens, the butter-making, and all the other jobs expected of a farmer's wife. Her energy put him to shame.

As he turned up the track towards Brookfield, he saw his father and young Philip coming out of the milking shed. They both looked pretty tired and Jack felt a pang of guilt. There'd been problems with a couple of the animals that morning, but when he'd offered to help his father had said he could manage. Jack hadn't insisted, and had gone off for his walk. Now he felt cross with himself that his father had obviously had to turn to Philip for help because he hadn't been around when he was needed.

Stamping the snow off his boots, he went into the kitchen. The two of them were already deep in conversation in front of the range and hardly noticed his arrival. Jack knew he was being unreasonable, but as happened so often these days, he felt a flash of anger against his younger brother. He was always being so obviously useful around the farm. Much more than Jack was.

Philip was a clever young beggar. Most of the village kids left school at fourteen, but he'd gone on to grammar school at Borchester and now there was talk of him going off to the Farming Institute for more education. It hadn't taken Jack long to realise he was wrong about the lad's value to his father. He seemed to spend half his time with his nose stuck in a farming magazine and the other trotting out the latest theories for increasing milk yields and going in for more and more mechanisation, but he was no shirker all the same. He revelled in rolling up his sleeves. The trouble was he was also beginning to get a bit cocky and once or twice he'd tried to tell Jack what to do and how to do it. He'd soon got a flea in his ear!

Jack wished the lad could be a bit more like their kid sister. Christine was a little smasher. She had a lovely nature and although she was every bit as smart as Philip, she never forced her cleverness down anyone's throat the way he did. She'd gone on to Borchester Grammar as well and was doing very well by all accounts, but she tended to share her bits of knowledge rather than flaunt them. When she told you things, there was always a sense of wonderment in her voice and you got the feeling she wanted you to know everything she knew rather than tell you how clever she was.

To be fair, both of them were very good to Peggy. Philip was always attentive and ready to take the heavier chores off her hands whenever she'd let him. Christine was clearly fascinated by the whole business of having a baby and several times he'd seen her with her ear pressed against Peggy's tummy, trying to hear the baby's heartbeat! They were like a pair of conspirators as they held regular whispered conversations about the baby's progress.

Jack still wasn't sure what it was going to be like to be a father. Everyone kept telling him about the sleepless nights and the endless nappy changing. He didn't know if he'd be expected to take his turn at any of that. He rather hoped not.

"Have you had a nice walk, Jack?"

As Peggy kissed him, he could smell the sweetness of the soap she'd used to wash her hair. He started to hug her but she gently pushed him away.

"Careful, Jack, don't forget the baby!"

"Forget it? How could I possibly forget it? You're getting as big as a mountain!"

She pretended to be upset.

"Well, ta ever so, Jack Archer. I love you too!"

He nuzzled her neck and she blushed and pushed him away again. Embarrassed, she glanced towards his mother and young Chris. He always forgot how shy she was.

"Sorry, love."

After they'd eaten, and the rest of the family had gone about their chores, Peggy washed up, clattering the dishes noisily in the sink. Jack sat and read the *Borchester Echo*. As usual, it was full of war news. He could have done without that. He was fed up with the constant reminders that there was still a war on.

Hanging the tea towel up neatly, Peggy came and perched precariously on the arm of Jack's chair and looking over his shoulder at the paper, she pointed to an advertisement for a "Gay Nineties Ball".

"Do you remember some of the dances we went to back in London? Wouldn't it be nice if we could go to that, Jack?"

She sounded a bit wistful. Jack was shocked. It was the first time Peg had even mentioned London since she'd been at Brookfield. Was she starting to feel homesick? There was nothing he could do about it even if she was. This was her home now.

"Don't be daft, lass. We can't go to a dance with you in your condition!"

To his relief, she giggled.

"I can't see you and me getting to a dance for a good few years now, Jack, but that doesn't stop me thinking it would be nice. Look, it's an all-woman band . . . that should be fun . . . and there are going to be demonstration dances by local nurses . . . and refreshments . . . all for five bob!"

She made five shillings sound like a paltry sum. Jack wondered what she would say if she knew he was earning less than four quid a week from his father? It wasn't much to keep a wife on, let alone a wife and child. Peggy noticed the frown pass across his face.

"What's the matter, Jack? Are you worried about what's going to happen when the baby's born?"

He looked at her for a moment. Should he burden her with all his worries about the future? Should he tell her about his haunting fear that he would never be able to offer her and the child a decent sort of life? He decided not to say anything to upset her.

"Of course, I'm looking forward to it. The little perisher's going to be our meal ticket when we get old and grey!"

She looked at him anxiously.

"What makes you think it's going to be a boy? What if it's a girl? Will you be very disappointed?"

"Disappointed? Well . . . I won't be disappointed if she turns out to look like you. In any case, who says a girl can't pay her way these days? After all the work women have been taking on to help the war effort, I reckon they'll be demanding the same wages as men before long!"

Peggy smiled to herself. Perhaps her propaganda had been getting through after all. It was only the other day she'd been pointing out to Jack how much farming owed to the two hundred thousand women in the Land Army who'd kept things going while the men were away fighting. Even so, he tried to stop her helping Doris with the chickens.

Peggy shifted uncomfortably on the arm of the chair, dislodging an envelope that was sticking out of her apron pocket. Bending to pick it up, Jack noticed the London postmark.

"A letter from your mother?"

Peggy looked at him guiltily.

"Yes . . . I forgot to mention it to you. It came this morning."

Jack regarded his relationship with his mother-in-law as fairly normal. They didn't really like each other. It was clear that Mrs Perkins thought he wasn't good enough for her daughter. He'd once overheard her complaining to a neighbour that he was only an

23

ordinary private while her Peg was a lance-corporal, and she'd been even more scathing when she'd described him, for no reason he could ever fathom, as a pig farmer.

Privately, he thought she was a bit of a harridan. Her sharp features seemed permanently set in a scowl as she complained endlessly about everything under the sun. She was also incredibly old-fashioned. She never went out without her long black coat on and she always insisted on wearing a hat, even when she was working about the house. Yet she only seemed to have one – a silly-looking thing it was, too, with black feathers sticking out of it!

He and Peggy had never talked about it much, but he suspected she had a pretty good idea of what his feelings about her mother were because she took good care not to bring her up in conversation too often.

"How is she?"

"She's fine!"

"And your dad?"

Albert Perkins was an even rummer character than his wife but, Jack thought, he probably had more excuse. Not only did he have to put up with Mrs P and all her funny little ways, he also suffered very bad health. In fact, Jack couldn't think why he'd been daft enough to ask how he was. He knew the answer already.

"I don't think he's very well. Mum says he's been keeping her up at night again with his coughing and spluttering. She says she hasn't had a decent night's sleep for weeks."

The old man ill and Mrs P complaining about him – that sounded more or less par for the course.

"What else has she got to say? Has she got over the idea of me kidnapping you and dragging you off to the back of beyond?"

Peggy shook her head and looked at him sadly.

"I really don't know why you should think that Mum sees it that way, Jack. She's really very fond of you. As

24

a matter of fact, she says in her letter that she's ever so glad I've escaped from the grime and dirt of London. She reckons I've done the right thing."

Jack looked at her in disbelief.

"You don't mean she's actually said you've done the right thing in marrying me?"

Mrs P had obviously entertained high hopes for her only daughter. Somehow, despite her husband's lack of a regular wage, she'd kept Peggy at school until she was sixteen. Whatever plans she'd had for her had then been knocked on the head by the war, and poor Peg had ended up as a dressmaker in a back-street sweatshop somewhere in the East End. But Mrs P's ambitions were raised again when her daughter joined the ATS and quickly won promotion. No wonder Peg's marrying Jack must have seemed like a comedown to her.

Peggy, of course, wasn't a bit like her mother, or her father, either. For one thing, she had very strong socialist views, unlike her mother and Jack too, come to that. She was always wishing that everyone was equal which Jack thought was a barmy theory.

"She doesn't go quite so far as to say you're Mr Right but she does say I'm dead lucky to be a farmer's wife. She says she quite fancies the idea of living in the country herself. As a matter of fact, Jack, she says she'd like to visit us once the baby's arrived."

He tried not to groan.

"What? Your mum come here to Brookfield?"

"Yes. Why not? Don't you think it's a good idea?"

"I'm not sure it is, love. All the fresh air up here would probably do for your dad."

"Oh, Dad wouldn't come . . . just Mum."

Jack wasn't sure whether or not that was much of a relief. Mrs P was more than enough to drive everyone in Ambridge mad.

"Where would she stay? We can hardly ask her to stay at Brookfield. Don't forget it's not our house, Peg."

"I think if you asked your mum about it, she'd be delighted. She's always saying she'd love to meet my mother."

Jack couldn't imagine two people with less in common than his mother and Mrs P. Doris was a quiet, gentle woman who loved nothing more than looking after her family, at her happiest with her sleeves rolled up, flour up to her elbows, and mountains of baking and cooking to be done. He could always tell when it was baking day at Brookfield because that was the day when Doris sang the loudest. She had a nice voice and sang in the church choir. That was the last thing he could imagine Mrs P doing. With her harsh, croaky voice, she'd frighten the dead. He couldn't see her getting stuck into all the kitchen chores without moaning and groaning about the housewife's lot either. No, the two of them would be like chalk and cheese together. Better not try it.

If his mother had told Peggy she'd like to meet Mrs P, it could only have been out of kindness. There couldn't possibly be any other reason! Not that he could say that to Peggy, of course.

"I think we should leave it until we've got a place of our own, Peg."

"But that could be ages. I would like to see her, you know. She is my mum and I do miss her. It would be lovely to have her around when the baby comes."

"I understand that, but it won't be all that long before we can get a cottage of our own and then you can have your mother to stay as often and as long as you like. Besides, my mum has told you she'll look after you when the time comes. You can't have the two of them fussing around."

Peggy recognised defeat. She'd never really expected Jack to agree to her mother coming to stay, and she gave in gracefully.

"You're right. I'm sorry to have made a fuss and I wouldn't want you to think I don't appreciate all that your mum's done for me already. I'll write and tell

Mum it's not convenient just yet. I'm sure she'll understand."

Jack was quietly congratulating himself on solving a tricky situation when his mother came into the kitchen in time to overhear Peggy's last remark.

"What's not convenient, Peggy?"

"Er . . . nothing in particular. Jack and I were just talking about waiting until we get a place of our own before inviting my mother up to Ambridge."

"Doesn't she want to come up before that? Wouldn't you like her to be here in time for the baby?"

Peggy saw Jack's mouth begin to tighten. She didn't know what to say so she just shrugged her shoulders. Doris Archer was shrewd enough to realise what had happened.

"Our Jack hasn't been saying you can't put your mum up here at Brookfield, has he?"

She didn't wait for an answer.

"Well, if he has, just you ignore him, Peggy. While you're under this roof, this is your home. It's ever so important you feel that it is, and if you want your mum to be with you when the baby comes, then she's more than welcome. There's plenty of room in the house and an extra pair of hands is always welcome at a time like that."

Overwhelmed by this rush of kindness, Peggy dissolved into tears. Doris gently put her arms round the young girl and turned to her bewildered-looking son.

"You can get off and help your dad, Jack. He could do with a hand. I don't think Simon's feeling too well and he's only working at half-pace."

In all the years that Simon Cooper had been the Brookfield farmhand, Jack had never known him to have a day's illness. His mother was just trying to get rid of him.

"But, Mum . . ."

"No buts, Jack. Off you go! Don't you worry about Peg. She's just a bit over-tired. She'll be all right shortly. I'll look after her."

27

Once Jack had gone off as told, Doris persuaded Peggy to wipe away her tears.

"Don't take any notice of our Jack, Peggy. Men are all the same . . . thoughtless! They don't understand what it's like to uproot yourself and leave your family to live in a strange place. They see themselves as the lord and master who will provide for their wife's every need . . . and if you need something they can't provide, like a mother's shoulder to cry on, it wounds their masculine pride."

Peggy had stopped sniffling, but Doris carried on.

"You'll learn, Peggy, that the best thing to do to get your own way is to pretend that you're not the slightest bit bothered one way or the other, and then you just watch how fast they come round. You see, they can feel then that it's them that's giving you what you want. It fits in with their image of themselves as the provider!"

Peggy was smiling almost broadly now.

"I'm sorry about crying, Mrs Archer . . ."

"Come on now, my girl. For the last time . . . it's not Mrs Archer. I'm Doris or Mum – whichever you prefer."

Peggy beamed.

"Maybe I could call you Mum Two?"

"Why, of course you can, my dear!"

"Only, you see . . . well . . . I know you've been ever so kind to me and I do appreciate it and I know I would never have survived here without you, but . . . well . . . I do have my own mum as well . . ."

"Oh Peg, love, don't be daft! I understand. I don't want to take the place of your mother. I just want you to feel at home here. I want you to be one of the family."

"That's very kind of you."

"I remember what it was like when I first came to Brookfield. Dan's mother was still alive and this was *her* home. When I moved in after getting married, I felt very much as if I was an intruder. I was always frightened to do anything because she could do it ever

28

so much better than me. But you know, Peg, I soon found out I was being unfair to her. She was a lovely woman and she wanted nothing more than to put me at my ease. In the end, it was her that taught me how to become a farmer's wife . . . so if there's anything I can do to help you, it'll just be like passing on a bit of the family inheritance."

Peggy looked as if she was going to burst into tears again.

"Oh, Mum, I do need your help. If you found it hard just try to think what it's like for me. At least you were brought up in the village, but I was born in the East End of London and that's a very different world from Ambridge."

"You mustn't think of places, Peg. It's people that make up this world and I'm sure you'll find the Ambridge folk are every bit as nice as your London friends and neighbours. Just give them a chance."

"But that's the trouble, Mum. Apart from the family and the odd word or two with Simon and the postman, I haven't spoken to another person since I arrived. Jack hasn't introduced me to anybody."

Doris patted her gently on the tummy.

"I think that's probably got a lot to do with it, don't you? Once the baby's arrived, you'll soon be out and about, and then I'm sure the villagers will take to you very quickly. You'll see."

"Are you sure?"

"Of course I am!"

"Only . . . in London, you see, the people who live in lodgings never seem to be part of the community. I think they're seen as rolling stones who are going to be passing on sooner or later, and it's hardly worth getting to know them."

"Ah, Peggy, I don't think you understand the country ways. You're not a lodger here . . . you're family. You can stay here as long as you like. Brookfield's your home, and you must feel free to invite your family or friends here whenever you want to. If you'd like your parents here for Christmas, just you invite them . . . and if our Jack tries to say anything different, you leave him to me."

The tears were rolling down Peggy's cheeks again.

"Oh Mum, I'm sorry for blubbering but it's not what you think. It's not that you and the family haven't made me feel at home. It's the exact opposite. You've been so kind – all of you, even young Philip and Christine – that I'm almost putting down roots already."

"Well, that's lovely . . ."

"No . . . no, it's not! I can't afford to. It wouldn't work for Jack. He's got all these plans for having his own tenancy and if he felt I was settled here at Brookfield, he'd think there was nothing to strive for. I don't want him to be able to blame me for not getting on. He already blames me for not going off to fight in the war."

Doris was lost.

"How could Jack possibly blame you for that?"

"He wants to believe that he'd eventually have been sent into action, and it was only me getting pregnant that stopped him."

"That's nonsense! It was his health that kept him back . . . and anyway, he should be grateful to have been spared all that."

Peggy shook her head. The tears had gone, but there was still an anxious look on her face.

"You really don't understand, Mum. It's terrible having to sit on the sidelines. It was bad enough for me, and I never expected to go to France or anywhere. But Jack desperately wanted to be in the fighting. He's really a hero under the skin, and he wanted nothing more than to win a medal and bring it back here like his Uncle Ben did in the last war."

Doris still wasn't sure she understood, but she was prepared to offer a sympathetic ear to her daughter-in-law. Peggy obviously needed to talk.

"You've got no idea what it was like for the boys on a home posting. They were so close to normal life and yet they were still far from it. They could go down the road to the local pub all right, but then have to put up with all the snide comments about their luck in having a cushy billet while the other lads went off to be killed. Then when the lads who had seen action came back and went to the same pub, they were treated like heroes and never had to buy a single drink for themselves."

Doris shook her head in bewilderment.

"You know, love, our Jack has never let on about anything like that. He's never said a word about any of it."

"I'm not surprised. He's not said anything to me either but I could see the effect it had on him with my own eyes. When he first came to Aldershot, he was just a bit put out at not making the Borsetshires but he was still reasonably cheerful. It was when the first lot went off to France without him that he started to change."

Doris got up to tighten the kitchen tap that had been dripping loudly into the sink.

"Men are daft, aren't they? Jack could have talked to Dan about any of his problems. Dan's been through it all himself in the Great War. He was all geared up to go into the front line but then his father died and he had to come back here to take over the tenancy of Brookfield. He could have told Jack all about those feelings. I remember him telling me how bitter he felt when his brother Ben had come back as a hero and rubbed Dan's nose in the dirt a bit."

Peggy looked even more anxiously at her mother-in-law.

"That's another one of Jack's worries. He knows all about the conflict between Dad and his brother and he's got a dread that history will repeat itself with him and young Philip."

"Good lord! He's not bothered about the lad, is he? He must be in a very bad way. He can't seriously feel threatened by young Phil?"

31

Peggy nodded.

"I'm afraid Jack feels threatened by everyone and everything at the moment. He's got it into his head that Phil's got a big start on him because he went to school until he was sixteen and now he's going to go on to the Farm Institute. He overheard Phil talking to his father about the lambing the other day. Jack says he came up with a grand idea that would cut down on the number of premature deaths or something – something to do with developing or making a little coat to keep out the cold, Jack said. I'm not quite sure. It didn't seem much to me but Jack was very impressed. But then he got very cross with himself because he hadn't thought of it first."

They were interrupted by the sound of heavy boots outside the kitchen door and Jack came in, looking very sorry for himself.

"I'm not needed out there and I'm obviously not wanted in here so I think I'll go for another walk."

His mother looked out of the window. It was still snowing heavily . . . enough to make her think there was going to be a white Christmas.

"Don't be daft, lad, you can't go out in this weather. Peg and I were just discussing names for the baby so you can stay and help her do the choosing."

Jack was still sulking and looked at his wife crossly.

"That won't take long. I've made up my mind . . . it's to be William Daniel Anthony!"

Doris smiled but Peggy looked worried yet again.

"But Jack, I've asked you before . . . what if it's not a boy? It's only a fifty-fifty chance, you know."

CHAPTER THREE

Jack couldn't quite take it in. After hours of pacing up and down outside the labour ward of Felpersham Cottage Hospital, the nurse had given him the news. He was a father. Peggy had just given birth to a bonny baby girl weighing a whopping seven and a half pounds.

During all the long discussions beforehand, Jack had been convinced he'd be bitterly disappointed if the baby wasn't a boy. He'd refused to consider that it might just be a girl. Even while he was puffing his way through a whole packet of Woodbines in the tiny waiting-room, he was sure he'd be heartbroken if it didn't turn out to be a son he could call William Daniel Anthony . . . Billy!

Now that the inconceivable had happened, he found to his surprise that he didn't mind in the slightest. The only thing that mattered was that he was a father. No . . . that wasn't true . . . what mattered most was that he and Peg were parents!

When the doctors had finished whatever it was they did on such occasions, and Jack was eventually allowed in to see her, Peggy was lying in bed looking very tired and weary. She'd only been taken to the hospital because the midwife had forecast a difficult birth, otherwise she'd have had the baby at Brookfield. In the end, the nurse had said a caesarian hadn't been necessary, but it had been a rough few hours for Peggy all the same. She still looked slightly feverish and could only manage a weak smile.

"I'm sorry to disappoint you, Jack, but if you're prepared to give me another chance, I'll try to do better next time round!"

Jack suddenly felt ashamed of himself. He'd obviously gone prattling on so much about having a son, that now he was preventing his wife from enjoying what should be one of the most important moments of her young life. He felt wretched.

"Peg, my love, don't say such things. Don't even think them. It's not your fault . . . that's daft. It's not anybody's fault. How can we be talking about blame when we've got the most beautiful baby in the world. Forgive me for making you feel like that. I'm not in the least bit disappointed . . . honestly I'm not. In fact, I can't remember the last time I felt so happy!"

He looked around furtively to see if anyone was watching and then leaned over and kissed her very gently.

"I've just remembered the last time I felt this way . . . it was when you said you'd be my wife!"

Great tears rolled down Peggy's cheeks.

"Oh, Jack, I'm so relieved! I thought you'd hate having another girl to look after. When the nurse told me, I even asked her if there hadn't been some mistake . . ."

Jack shook his head.

"Why? Because Jack Archer had ordered a boy, is that what you told her? I bet she had a sharp answer to that . . . 'Who the hell does this Jack Archer think he is? He'll have a girl and like it!' Well, she's right. I do like it. In fact, old girl, I think it's fantastic!"

They sat holding hands looking happily into each other's eyes just as they had done when they first realised they were in love, content not to talk for a few minutes. Peggy had never seen Jack in such a thoughtful and considerate mood. Maybe she was right after all in thinking she could help him to wipe away some of the bitterness of his army experiences. Over the past weeks she'd begun to have some very serious doubts about that. He'd become so reluctant to do anything on the farm, and she'd noticed that he'd been drinking even more than usual. Now she put all that out of her mind.

"What about a name then? We never did get round to discussing it properly and somehow I don't think William Daniel Anthony is quite right, do you? Have you got any bright ideas? What about calling her after your mum?"

Jack shook his head.

"I don't think so, Peg. We can't call a little baby Doris, can we? And before you say it, I don't think your mum's got the right monicker either. Polly's fine for a parrot!"

The first time Jack had met Mrs Perkins she'd been wearing her feathered hat and he'd said she reminded him of a bleeding parrot. To his relief, Peggy laughed. She always did when he used any of her Cockney words. She let her own accent rip.

"Wot you gonna call her then, mate? She's gotta 'ave an 'andle, ain't she?"

Jack was delighted to see how quickly his little Cockney sparrow had regained her chirpy spirits. She was looking brighter and more cheerful than he'd seen her for ages.

"What about Lilian? After that other ATS corporal at Aldershot?"

"Wot? The blonde you kept giving the glad-eye to when you thought I wasn't looking? No fear."

"But it's a nice name . . ."

"Blimey mate, we can't call her that. Down in London she'd be Lil in no time at all. I ain't 'aving that. You'll 'ave to fink of something else."

Jack grinned. He thought for a moment. What about that wireless programme they both listened to where one of the characters kept asking "What's your name little girl?" Trouble was, he couldn't remember the answer. Then it came to him . . . a sweet little voice saying "My name's Jennifer!"

"What would you say to Jennifer, my girl? Your Cockney pals would find it hard to mess about with a smart name like that. It's just right to go with a name like Archer. Jennifer Archer . . . it's got a nice ring about it, don't you fink . . . blimey, I mean think!"

Peggy smiled and nodded in agreement, and promptly came up with the next line of the show's patter.

"That's a nice name for a little girl!"

35

They both laughed happily and Jack gave the proud mother another hug.

"That's it then . . . Jennifer it is . . . and we won't let anybody shorten it to Jenny."

The nurse came and took him to see the baby . . . a tiny little bundle of red wrinkles and a great mop of jet black hair. Jack gazed at her in awe. He'd never seen a newborn baby before. It wasn't a bit like he'd expected.

"Er . . . is it all right?

The nurse looked at him in amused surprise.

"All right? She's a lovely girl."

"But it . . . I mean she's ever so small."

"I tell you what, Mr Archer, if it had been you that had given birth to this beauty you wouldn't think she was so small. Seven and a half pounds is plenty big enough to be going on with."

On the way back to Brookfield, Jack Archer firmly resolved to turn over a new leaf and to take his new responsibility as a father very seriously. He'd start by working harder on the farm. He knew he hadn't really been pulling his weight. Once or twice he'd suspected that Peggy had been about to tell him off for sponging off his parents, but each time he'd turned very gruff and managed to stop her before she could say anything.

The trouble was, his father had got the farm into such good shape there wasn't much he could think of to do by way of improvement. He'd thought about suggesting putting more land down to corn but they already had forty acres and that was more than enough for the time being. He'd just been going to say they could do with another odd acre or two of winter barley and wheat when his father had said exactly the same thing. Very frustrating that had been.

Any other ideas he'd had always seemed very basic compared with young Philip's constant monologue about mechanisation and modernisation. Jack didn't know what he was talking about half the time, but when it came to saving sweat and being more efficient, he had to admit the lad had a point. That's something else he resolved to do from now on . . . listen to the lad.

At home, everyone was delighted with the news. His mother burst into tears, and was promptly joined by little Christine. His father shook his hand firmly and then gave him an uncharacteristic hug. Even Philip was openly pleased, and there was nothing Smart Alec about him as he offered a grown-up handshake and a great slap on the back.

When she had stopped crying, his mother asked him if he'd let Mrs Perkins know.

"Heck, no. I clean forgot all about that. I suppose I ought to send her a wire."

"Aye, you should . . . and don't forget to add an invitation to Brookfield as soon as she can make it."

Jack was happy to agree and Doris didn't let on that she'd already sent an invitation to Mrs Perkins and was expecting her at Brookfield within the next couple of days anyway.

Later, when all the family congratulations and celebrations had subsided, Dan quietly slipped Jack a pound note and suggested he went down to The Bull to wet the baby's head with his mates. He accepted the money gratefully but, for once, didn't rush straight off.

When he eventually got to the pub, it was very busy. Half the men in the village seemed to be there, and all the conversation was about a forthcoming football match . . . a derby with a tough Birmingham team.

Jack wasn't sure how far his few bob would go if he offered to stand a round for everyone but he needn't have worried. His announcement that he'd just become a father was greeted with a great roar of approval, and Sam Crowcroft, the landlord, got an even bigger cheer when he said the next round was on the house.

The next one was bought by his uncle, Tom Forrest, the local gamekeeper, and the one after that by Bob

Larkin, one of the local poachers! Jack couldn't keep track after that, but for the rest of the evening no one would let him put his hand in his pocket.

In between drinks, the conversation reached sophisticated levels.

"Tell us how you did it then Jack!"

"Didn't think you had it in you."

"I thought you were off fighting the Jerries, not having a good time round the back of the Naafi!"

"Don't you have to do it by numbers in the army?"

A few days earlier, Jack would have been upset by any mention of his army career but this evening he didn't care. He had more important things to think about. So had most of the other men in the bar. Their main concern tonight was the football match.

Farmer George Grundy was Ambridge team manager and by a series of minor miracles, he'd managed to steer his team into the third round of the regional challenge cup. They'd never got beyond the first round before, mainly because the teams from the big towns were able to field two or three semi-professionals from the factories. But with so many men in the forces, most teams were struggling to field a regular eleven.

So far luck had been on George Grundy's side, and he'd been able to hold together eleven players for most of the season. But now, with the big match only a couple of weeks away, he was in trouble. He couldn't get a side together.

"How many are we short of, George?"

"I'm not sure yet, but it could be as many as three or four."

"We'll never be able to find that many."

"That's what I keep telling you. We might as well scratch now. We can't turn out a sub-standard side . . . not against Stirchley."

Stirchley had won the cup in the previous two years, and when they'd last played Ambridge they'd hammered them seven-nil.

"Have they still got that young bloke Woolley playing for them?"

"Yes. They're playing him at centre-forward now."

"How come he's not been called up then?"

Jack Woolley, Stirchley's leading goal-scorer, was a burly teenager who used weight rather than skill to crash his way through opposing defences.

"We could use beggars like that against Hitler's tanks!"

George Grundy got fed up with all the banter.

"Hasn't anyone got any bright ideas?"

Tom Forrest, once a fleet-footed left-winger but now one of the veterans of the team who'd been reduced to playing left back, suggested George might have to turn out himself. The idea didn't go down well. George was nearly sixty, and anyway his sport was really cricket. He only looked after the football team because it meant the odd free pint or two from lads who wanted to get into the team.

"Don't be bloody daft, Tom Forrest. I wouldn't even know how to lace up those stupid boots you have to wear."

Jack was bemused by the discussion. Before he went off to join the army, there'd always been fierce competition to play for the village team. At school he'd fancied himself a bit on the field but he'd never been good enough to make the village side.

"Why are you so short of players, George?"

"Why? I'll tell you why . . . because no one cares about village pride any more. When I was a lad . . ."

A great roar of laughter went up, cutting off George's notorious reminiscences in their prime. It was Tom Forrest who took the present discussion in hand. Despite his age, he still took his football very seriously and he was determined to help George get a team sorted out.

"Come on now, lads. George is right. It's the pride of the village that's at stake. We've got to turn out a respectable side against this Brummagem lot. I reckon we could have the beating of them this year."

Sam Crowcroft, who could see valuable drinking time disappear if the problem wasn't sorted out, added his twopenn'orth.

"Let's see who we're actually short of, George. Who've you got playing for definite already?"

George Grundy took a piece of paper from his jacket pocket and carefully unfolded it on the table so that those who wanted to could look over his shoulder.

"Well, there's no goalkeeper for a start. Joe Dunnington's hurt his back and won't be right for another couple of weeks."

Joe was the village blacksmith. Half the men in the pub knew to their cost that he was injured because they hadn't been able to get any horses shod for the past week and more.

"Tom's all right at left back, and if I can get my lazy son off his backside, he'll play at right back."

Joe Grundy was supposed to work Grange Farm with his father, but there was always a running dispute between them over what constituted work. Joe argued that if you got what you paid for, his old man wasn't entitled to more than an hour or two's effort a day. If it hadn't been for George's long-suffering wife, Susan, there would probably have been bloodshed at Grange Farm before now.

Tom Forrest looked anxiously at the piece of paper.

"I hope the vet's all right at right half. We'd be really sunk without him. I reckon as how he's got the beating of Stirchley in his own two boots."

Ian Robertson, Ambridge's young Scottish vet, had played for Glasgow's famous amateur side, Queen's Park, when he'd been at university there.

"Aye, it's all right. Mr Robertson's fit enough, but we've got to make sure none of you farmers drag him away from the game with some trumped up emergency. That's what happened two or three weeks ago, and he only got back on the pitch with a couple of minutes left to play!"

There were muttered assurances that no such thing would happen this time and Bert Garland, who'd been the culprit on that occasion, hurriedly moved on down the list.

"Larkin at centre-half! Bloody hell, George. You can't put that old codger there. Have you seen him lately? I reckon he's just about kept together by that bit of string that holds up his trousers!"

Tom Forrest bridled.

"Hang on a minute. Ned Larkin's no old codger. He might look like one but he's no more than a few months older than me. I hope you're not suggesting that I've got one foot in the grave?"

Tom was still a few years short of his fortieth birthday, but Bert Garland was unrepentant.

"No offence to you, Tom, but I reckon Mabel Larkin hasn't been feeding Ned properly or something. He certainly looks decrepit."

George let him finish before looking at him with contempt. Ned Larkin had been a fairly useful player in his day, but he hadn't been on a football pitch for ten years or more.

"Don't be dafter than you can help, Bert Garland. That's not Ned Larkin down there. That's his nipper, Jethro."

Jack remembered Jethro Larkin. He was a spindly-legged little lad who, he was sure, couldn't be more than thirteen or fourteen.

"Do you think it's safe to put a kid like that up against the Brummies? They're likely to knock ten bells out of him."

"They are not! You can't have clapped eyes on the lad since you got back from the war . . ."

"I wasn't in the war!"

"All right, all right . . . since you got back from the army. He's a strapping lad now and can hold his own with anyone. Isn't that right, Tom?"

Tom nodded in agreement.

"He's a tough beggar for a seventeen-year-old. There's no need to worry on his account."

"How are your two lads set, Jess?"

George Grundy called over to Jess Allard who was sitting on his own, away from the main group, not taking any part in the discussion. He had problems on his farm and football was the last thing on his mind just now.

"Set for what, George?"

"Are Joe and Rex available for the cup match against Stirchley?"

"I'm blessed if I know, but if it means the lazy beggars get an afternoon off work, I'm sure they'll be there."

"Well, I'll put them down for certain . . . so that takes care of inside left and the left wing, but I'm stuck with the other three positions. What do you think about asking Bob Larkin to play at centre-forward, Tom?"

A hush fell over the bar as everyone turned to watch Tom Forrest's face. Ned Larkin's younger brother had the reputation of being the most notorious poacher in the district, but so far Tom had never been able to catch him in the act. There was certainly no love lost between the two.

"I'd be a darn sight happier if we could have Jim Harris there as usual. What's wrong with him?"

George shrugged his shoulders.

"There's no use hoping for the impossible. I've already tried Jim, of course, but he's not going to be available for a couple of weeks. His sister's got diphtheria or something and the family's being put into isolation."

"What? Young Prue's got diphtheria? I can't believe that. I saw her just the other day and she was fine then."

After the ribbing they'd given him about Bob Larkin, no one said anything about Tom's obvious concern for Prue Harris. She sometimes helped out in the bar when Sam Crowcroft was short-handed and although she was a good fifteen years younger than Tom, he was known by everyone there to be sweet on her. Not that he'd ever admit it though!

"You talk to Dr Harvey if you don't believe me, Tom. Anyway, we still haven't solved the problem of centre-forward. What do you say to Bob Larkin?"

Tom knew he was in a corner. His better nature won through.

"If Larkin's the only one available, then you'd better play him. It'll give my birds an afternoon off anyway!"

There was general laughter at Tom's reply.

After a good deal more wrangling and discussion, George managed to fill the other two forward positions at last. Ginger Green, the poultryman on the Fairbrother estate, went in as right-winger and Harry Cobb, the village handyman, was put down at inside right. That left only the goalkeeper's jersey to be filled. Names were tossed backwards and forwards – Jim Price, the postman; one or two farmers, including Bill Sawyer, who everyone reckoned *was* nearing his dotage; even a couple of teenagers, Nelson Gabriel and Philip Archer.

That made Jack sit up. Through the alcoholic haze induced by five pints of ale, he suddenly realised that no one had mentioned him as a possible member of the team and he felt peeved. If they thought young Nelson Gabriel and even his kid brother were worth mentioning, why not him? He had a track record . . . of sorts.

"I used to play a lot of football when I was at school."

George Grundy looked at him with new interest.

"What about that chest of yours?"

"What do you mean?"

"Don't you have a wheezy chest? Isn't that what your dad said kept you out of active service?"

"That was nothing . . . just some incompetent MO with wax in his ruddy ears. There's nothing wrong with me!"

"Hang on, lad, I'm not saying that there is. I was just asking a question. As manager of the team, I've got a responsibility you know. It'd never do for me to ask anyone to put themselves at any kind of risk just for a game of football."

Bert Garland, who'd been listening with growing impatience, couldn't contain himself.

"Don't be so ruddy pompous, George Grundy. If the lad wants to volunteer his services, I say as how you ought to give him a chance! Seems to me that you don't have too many options anyway."

There were general murmurs of approval.

"Aye, let him have a go!"

"If he wants to play and he's not fit that's his look-out."

"We can't field ten players."

George Grundy didn't really have any objection to Jack playing but in his usual pig-headed way he'd got himself into a corner, and the only way out was to bluster.

"He'll have to have a trial. I'm not putting him, or anybody else, into the team without seeing how he looks in a football jersey!"

The argy-bargy could have gone on all night if Sam Crowcroft hadn't intimated that he was about to close the pub. In the end, George and Jack hurriedly agreed that the matter should be settled during a practice knockabout the following Saturday afternoon.

At breakfast next morning, Jack told his father what had happened. He thought Dan would be pleased that he was taking a part in village affairs, but he was horrified to be reminded that Peggy was due to bring the baby out of the cottage hospital on Saturday . . . at two o'clock!

"Oh, help! Now what do I do? I can't back down after making such a fuss about being picked."

His father was not sympathetic.

"Well, your mum and I will happily fetch Peg and the baby from Felpersham but I suspect she won't be best pleased to find you not there because you're off playing a silly game of football."

His mother was not only unsympathetic – she was furious.

"You've got to get a grip on yourself, my lad. You seem to forget you're a married man with responsibilities now. I've not heard anything as daft as this notion of you playing football for many a long year. It's the drink that's done it. You just go and tell George Grundy and that brother of mine that you've got better things to do on Saturday afternoon than chase a football around. I'm surprised at our Tom. He's usually got more sense than that. Wait until I see him!"

Jack knew his mother was right, but there had been too many people in The Bull for him to try and pull out of what would effectively be a trial of his general fitness. It wasn't just about football. It was about proving something . . . that he was as strong as the next man . . . that the army had got it wrong . . . that he was a man!

"If I'm going to be able to walk through this village with my head in the air, I've got to be there on Saturday. I'll explain it to Peg. She'll understand."

Doris Archer wanted to shake her eldest son. Sometimes he could be very pig-headed.

"You talk to him, Dan. Tell him that his wife and baby are more important than his silly pride. Go on, tell him."

Dan was hesitant. There was no doubt that Jack had got himself into a fix, but Dan knew exactly where he got his stubborn streak from. He himself had been accused of being pig-headed on many an occasion.

"I think we should give it a rest now. He'll know better what to do when he's had time to chew it over."

Things didn't get any clearer though. The more he thought about it, the more Jack felt he had to go through with the football trial. His mother was furious that he could even consider it. In the end, it was Dan who hit on a diplomatic solution.

"What if we could persuade the hospital to let Peg and the baby out in the morning?"

Doris stoutly refused to have any part of it, so Dan spoke to Ian Robertson who spoke to Dr Harvey who spoke to the hospital matron. Although she nearly had apoplexy at the very suggestion that her routines should be disrupted, the doctor's bedside manner proved as effective with her as it did with his patients.

Dan drove Jack to Felpersham on the Saturday morning and Peggy and little Jennifer were brought safely back to Ambridge. No one enlightened Peggy about all the fuss that had been going on. In fact, she was delighted when Jack told her he was supposed to play football in the afternoon.

"That's marvellous, Jack. I'm so pleased you're going to get involved with village life again. I'm sure you'll come through the trial match with flying colours."

To everyone's surprise (including his own) he did, emerging from the game as a useful-looking goal-keeper.

George Grundy was able to congratulate him without a hint of resentment in his voice.

"You played a blinder lad!"

When Jack told Peggy later what he'd said she smiled from ear to ear.

"I knew you could do it!"

He only wished his daughter, wrapped up snugly in her cot, could have understood too!

On the day of the cup-tie, Peggy was among the crowd of nearly a hundred supporters who turned out to watch the match. It was still bitterly cold and there was a thick layer of frost on the pitch as the players lined up for the whistle. Stirchley turned out to be a rough bunch and the referee was constantly in action, trying to stop tempers from getting frayed. George Grundy bawled himself hoarse as he bombarded his players with a stream of expletives mixed with instructions.

In the first half-hour, Jack was called upon to make more than a dozen saves although none of the shots were particularly threatening. As predicted, most of the danger came from the Birmingham team's burly centre-forward. Young Jack Woolley thundered around the pitch without concern for himself or his opponents. He reckoned every loose ball should be his and he went for it in no uncertain manner.

Just before half-time, the Stirchley winger made a long run down the right side of the field and then lofted in a dangerous-looking cross. Jack Archer could see the centre-forward storming into the penalty area, but he ignored him and leapt up to snatch the ball out of the air.

As Peggy and the Ambridge supporters gave a great cheer, Jack Woolley found he couldn't stop his charge on the slippery surface and he crashed full pelt into the helpless goalkeeper. There was a sickening thud and as Jack Archer rolled over, he felt a sharp pain in his left leg. Just before blacking out, he calmly realised that it was broken.

Later that night, when the pain had subsided and he looked at the gleaming white cast that had been put on at Felpersham Cottage Hospital, Jack Archer felt oddly comforted. As he'd been carried off the pitch, he'd heard George Grundy describe him as a bloody hero. The football pitch in Ambridge might not rate with the battlefields of France or North Africa, but Jack reckoned his broken leg was the next best thing to the medal he'd hoped for when he'd put on his army uniform.

CHAPTER FOUR

Tom Forrest and his little band of bell-ringers had never had a happier task. It was one minute past midnight on Tuesday, 8 May 1945. The war with Germany was finally over. After six long wearying years of conflict, peace in Europe had been declared as the strokes of midnight faded away. No one had dared to celebrate a minute too soon, but now, at long last they could say it was over. Tom Forrest had already taken the mufflers off the bells of St Stephen's Church and now, as his ringers swung into action, their clear tones could be heard all over the district, linking up with the bells of Penny Hassett and Loxley Baratt and all the other parishes throughout the land, joining in the clamouring celebrations that stretched from Land's End to John o'Groat's.

In Ambridge there was not a man, woman or child who wasn't involved in the celebrations that were going on in every corner of the village. At Brookfield Farm, young Philip Archer had organised a huge bonfire on behalf of the Young Farmers Club, and more than a hundred people were gathered around it, singing and dancing in the bright glow of the crackling flames.

Doris Archer had set out a table in the big barn loaded with all the food and drinks she could lay her hands on, and a barrel of beer had been propped up on the back of a hay-cart for the menfolk to help themselves. Now she bustled among the crowd urging everyone to eat and drink up. There was no need to stint themselves now that the war was over.

Slightly apart from the rest, Jack Archer stood gazing at the flames and observing the merriment. He had a pint of ale in one hand and his other arm was round Peggy's shoulders. She held the baby up, well wrapped against the cool night air, to admire the flames.

"Isn't it fantastic, Jack! It's all over at last. Just think – our lads won't be lining up at Aldershot any more to be kitted out to be killed."

Jack hugged her a little harder.

"Aye, it is grand, Peg."

Pleased as he was that the war was finally over, Jack wished all the same that the fuss of the celebrations could be done with. Somehow it seemed to be opening up all the old psychological wounds again. For the past few months, since he'd broken his leg in fact, he'd begun to enjoy some peace of mind. It had been a nasty injury that had taken a long time to mend and had left him with a slight limp, but it had given him a status in the village too. People in the street, as he had taken his first cautious walk down to The Bull, leaning heavily on a stick he'd borrowed from Dan, had come up and clapped him on the shoulder and said how brave he'd been in helping Ambridge to beat the Stirchley football team – and he'd revelled in the attention.

Such glory, however, was proving transitory. Now that the talk was of the real war again, of real heroism, there was no place for Jack Archer. He had played no part in that reality. He felt exposed, naked of medals, a nobody in the pages of the war's history.

"I think we ought to get the baby back to the house now, Peg."

"Oh no, Jack. She's fine. I've got her well wrapped up and she's fast asleep. Let's stay and enjoy the bonfire for a little while longer. Please!"

Jack drained his tankard without finding pleasure in the foaming beer.

"You stay if you want, but I'm going off to bed. I've had enough of all this, thank you very much."

Peggy didn't notice the sharpness in his voice. She was savouring the camaraderie of the celebrations, but glad as she was to be part of it, she couldn't help wondering a little wistfully what they would be up to at home. She knew the East Enders would be celebrating in their own way – they'd suffered too long from the

49

German bombing raids not to be exploding with pleasure tonight. If she knew anything, no one in London would go to sleep that night until every barrel of beer in the city had been drained dry!

It was several minutes before she realised that Jack had gone, but his father had watched him slip away from the party and make his way back towards the farmhouse.

"What's the matter with our Jack then, love?"

"What do you mean?"

"Why has he sloped off so early?"

"I'm not sure, Dad. I hadn't really noticed he'd gone."

"It's not like him to turn his back on an ale barrel that's far from empty! Is his leg playing him up again?"

"Not that I know of. I'd better go and see if he's all right."

Jack was sitting in the dark kitchen in front of the glow from the range, a tumbler of whisky in his hand.

"Are you all right, Jack?"

He didn't answer.

"What is it?"

"Put the baby in her cot and come and sit with me, Peg. I need you."

She hurried upstairs and settled little Jennifer down for the night. Back in the kitchen, she found Jack pouring another large measure of Scotch into his glass.

"Aren't you hitting the hard stuff a bit heavy tonight, Jack?"

He swung round sharply and for a moment she thought he was going to shout at her.

"What difference does . . . oh, never mind. I'm sorry, Peg. I just feel pretty miserable at the moment and I thought the whisky might help to dull the pain a bit."

Peggy looked at him with a growing anxiety. She knew from her experience of living in the rough, tough East End that the more a wife nagged her husband about drinking, the more likely the man was to go on hitting the bottle, so although she'd been aware of Jack's frequent resort to alcohol when they'd first returned to Ambridge, she'd kept quiet about it. Her patience seemed to have paid off. Since the football match Jack had really seemed to be throwing off the habit – she thought it was because he was so much more part of village life now. Tonight was the first time she'd seen him drinking whisky for weeks.

She knew the pain he was trying to dull had nothing to do with his broken leg, and she was almost scared to ask him about it.

"Do you want to talk?"

Jack swirled the Scotch around in the glass and sat staring into it before taking another gulp.

"I'm not sure that there is anything to say, Peg. It's just this war business . . ."

"But it's all over now."

"Over for who, Peg? Is it over for Irene Jenkins?"

Irene Jenkins was the girl who worked as receptionist for Dr Harvey. She was a lovely girl, very popular around the village because she used to deliver half the doctor's prescribed medicines personally, wobbling cheerfully along on her old bicycle. No one had seen her for about a fortnight . . . since the news came through that her husband had been killed in action somewhere in Holland.

"How do you think she must be feeling now? Her man lost only a few weeks from the end of the war . . . what a waste! What the hell did he die for?"

Peggy knew there was little she could do to ease Jack's troubled mind. She moved across to him and sat on his knee. She wanted to snuggle up to him and stop him talking, but he seemed more interested in his glass of whisky.

"Think about that lass in Borchester we read about in the paper not so long ago . . . the one who's been in hospital since her husband was killed in Italy. It said it was only his second day in action. What was his name? Lieutenant Hawkins, wasn't it? Of the Borsetshires.

Probably joined up about the same time as me, only he didn't get booted off the active service list by some jumped-up twerp of a doctor. They gave him a medal posthumously . . . bloody terrific. What do you think that did for his wife? Same age as you, near enough. What's she going to do for the rest of her life? What if she never recovers?"

Peggy didn't say anything. She was thinking about the poor man who'd been living in a little hut he'd built for himself in Lyttleton Cover on the other side of the village since the blitz on Coventry. He'd come back from work to find that a bomb had fallen on his house, destroying it completely, and his wife inside. He'd been so shocked that he'd just walked away, without even waiting for her body to be recovered.

He was a harmless soul and the villagers left him alone to live exactly as he wanted. He did a few odd jobs now and then, but mostly he lived off herbs and berries and birds' eggs. Close as his hut was to Tom Forrest's cottage, he also managed to do a bit of poaching – it was obvious that the hardened gamekeeper was prepared to turn a blind eye in his case. Every now and again he'd disappear for a week or two. People said he'd go back to Coventry in case his wife had been found safe and well after all, just to check up. Each time he came back he'd be just that little bit sadder. Peggy couldn't deny it: Jack was right . . . for lots of people the war would never be over.

Jack was still talking.

"And what about the so-called heroes? Are they going to be given special treatment after what they've done for their King and country? Are they, bloody hell?! You think about the last time. What happened to men like my Uncle Ben? Everyone said he was a hero and the village band turned out to welcome him home . . . and then what? Nothing. Not even his brother could put out a hand . . ."

"Jack – that's your dad you're talking about . . ."

"I know, and that's what makes it all seem so futile. If my own dad couldn't look after his brother, what hope is there? And what about Percy Hood . . . crawled through the mud to save some jumped-up officer and nearly had his legs blown off . . . what's his reward? He's reduced to selling cakes and buns in a scruffy little baker's shop. Then there's George Grundy . . . he was even a sergeant major in the Borsetshires, and served in France and Palestine as well. All he came back to was a broken-down holding that's hardly fit to be called a farm."

Peggy knew that Jack's bitterness stemmed from his own inability to find a decent place for himself and his family. When they'd first come back, he'd boasted about getting a farm tenancy soon enough. When that didn't happen, he'd said they'd find a smallholding. Now he'd settled for a cottage of their own, but even that hadn't turned up yet.

"You mustn't let things get you down so much, Jack. Try and think of all the good things. We've got each other . . . or isn't that enough?"

Sometimes she felt Jack wasn't happy being married to her. She knew that her city upbringing meant she didn't always understand country ways, although she hoped she was learning fast enough with Doris Archer's gentle guidance. But there were bound to have been times when she'd let him down.

She'd seen him one day in the village laughing and joking with Elsie Catcher, the very pretty teacher at the local school, and someone had let slip since that they'd once been sweethearts . . . before Jack went into the army. Perhaps they would have married if it hadn't been for the war. Elsie was country born and bred, and she would clearly have made a better farmer's wife than Peggy.

Despite her momentary doubts, though, Peggy Archer wasn't going to let anything like that get her down. She already had Jack, so there was nothing Elsie Catcher could do about it!

Jack still hadn't answered her question.

"I said, Jack . . . we've got each other. Isn't that a good thing?"

"Of course it is Peg, but . . ."

"No buts, Jack. Think what else you've got . . . a lovely little daughter, smashing parents, a great little brother and sister, a job. What more could you possibly want?"

"I want us to have somewhere to call our own."

"That'll come one day, Jack."

"I wish I had your confidence!"

"So do I, Jack, because it's only self-confidence you're lacking. Dad's ever so pleased with the way you've built up the dairy herd and I know he's relieved that all the fences have been repaired at long last. He says you're doing a grand job now. Why not talk about all that instead of being down all the time?"

"Has Dad really said he's pleased with me?"

"Of course he has, and he was saying only a couple of days ago that he's going to need you even more when Philip goes off to the Farming Institute . . ."

"Oh great! That's ruddy marvellous! I can actually fill in for my kid brother while he goes off to get even more education? That's terrific for my morale! Whatever you say, Peg, I know Dad doesn't really want to rely on me. I bet you anything you like he'll end up bringing in someone else to help Simon. You'll see."

Peggy looked at him guiltily. She knew that Dan had in fact already been talking to Ned Larkin about the possibility of him doing some work around Brookfield. She decided to change the subject.

"If you feel so strongly about things, Jack, why don't you do something about it?"

"Like what? What the hell more can I do? You know I've done everything to try and get a place sorted out!"

"I know you have, love. I wasn't really talking about that. You have done your best there and nobody's saying otherwise. I was thinking more about the world in general. You don't seem particularly happy with that."

"Of course I'm not. The whole system's rotten, but what do you expect me to do about it?"

"Well, you certainly won't do anything just sitting and talking about it here. You ought to join one of the political parties."

Peggy wanted to suggest he joined the Labour Party but she wasn't really sure what Jack's feelings were. Like most farmers, he was probably fairly conservative. She just didn't know, because they'd never talked about politics. Back at home they were discussed all the time – Clem Attlee was a local hero after all – but she'd never heard a single word about politicians, except for good old Winnie, in the months she'd been at Brookfield.

Peggy thought back to the last general election. She'd still been at school, but she'd got caught up in the excitement of it all, going to listen to some of the street-corner meetings. Once she'd even handed out leaflets for the Labour candidate. When the Spanish Civil War had broken out she'd dreamed of going off to join the International Brigade to show solidarity with their socialist comrades, as many of the union leaders in the docks had urged, but of course she was far too young and the wrong sex! How angry she'd been. Suddenly she realised exactly how Jack was feeling. Locked out by a system he couldn't control, just as she had been.

"Aren't you interested in politics, Jack?"

"I've never thought about it. Doesn't seem much point. They're all the same, these beggars. The Labour Party hasn't a cat in hell's chance of winning the election, that's for sure. Winnie will call it at exactly the right time to suit the Tories and he won't have to remind us how he won the war. Even your friend Attlee can't deny that."

Peggy was currently keeping her fingers crossed that the election wouldn't come before her twenty-first birthday in November. But all the signs indicated that Churchill planned to go to the country much sooner than that, as Jack said. He would want to take advantage of having won the war and he certainly wasn't going to worry about depriving Peggy Archer of her chance of voting.

"I think he could deny it, but I doubt if the Tory press will give him much of a chance. My grandfather always says they're happier to print half-truths because they take up less space than the whole truth!"

"It's got nothing to do with the papers. There's no way the British people will vote against Churchill. They'll never forget what he's done for the country. I reckon if George the Sixth wasn't such a nice bloke, they'd want to make Winnie king!"

Peggy laughed, but she had to confess Jack probably wasn't far wrong!

The next morning, the discussion around the breakfast table was again about politics – this time the politics of farming. Young Philip Archer was holding the floor on his usual favourite topic.

"I tell you, Dad, the way things are going we'll have to mechanise or we'll be left behind. When I was doing my interviews for the Farming Institute, the people there were saying it was only a matter of time before we'd have to give up horses and go over to tractors completely."

Jack groaned. His younger brother was on his hobbyhorse yet again. Peggy grinned because she enjoyed Phil's youthful enthusiasm. Admittedly, she didn't know whether or not he was spouting a lot of rubbish, but he made it sound interesting and it certainly got the rest of the family going.

Dan Archer carefully buttered another piece of toast. He didn't want to put his younger son down, but he was fed up with being told how to run his farm.

"Don't you think you should wait until after you've been to the Institute before you spend so much time pontificating about this great new future you see for us all?"

Philip had gone to bed much later than everyone else in the house but his personal celebrations hadn't involved the consumption of the same amount of ale as his father or Jack. He was feeling much more lively than either of them.

"Come on, Dad. Don't be a Luddite. You can't stand in the way of progress. It'll just knock you over."

This was too much for Dan . . . especially with his head throbbing the way it was.

"I'm no ruddy Luddite. I'll have you know, young Philip, I've been running this farm for nigh on thirty years now without your advice and I'm not sure as how I want to have too much of it right now. Progress isn't going to run me over. I'm all in favour of progress, but you've got to let it happen all in its own good time."

Philip was nothing if not reckless.

"But, Dad, you're not letting anything happen. You wouldn't even let any of those Land Army girls come on to the farm because you thought they weren't up to the job. Well they've proved you wrong, haven't they?"

"For your information, young man, the reason those girls didn't come to Brookfield was purely practical. I told the Borchester Land Army office that I'd be more than happy to take one, maybe two at a push, because that's all we had work for here. They didn't want to know. They said the girls preferred to work on bigger farms where they could be in groups. It was much better for them that way, they said."

Philip was unabashed.

"Well you can't use that argument about tractors."

"I'm not using any argument about tractors. I've got a pair of fine horses and I intend to go on using them as long as I feel like it. Those two beasts can cope with all the awkward bumps and troughs around the place. You put a tractor to some of them and it'll just topple over on you."

"Oh, Dad, you're sounding like some antediluvian peasant now. Come into the twentieth century, for goodness sake."

Like Peggy, Doris Archer had been sitting on the sidelines listening to the argument with amusement. But she wasn't going to tolerate her son being rude to his father.

"Don't you talk to your father like that, young Philip. There's no call for that kind of talk in this house and you're still not too old to get a clip round the ear."

"I'm sorry, Mum . . . Dad. I didn't mean to be rude. It's just that I think maybe being so close to things it's sometimes difficult to see the wood for the trees!"

Jack laughed. His kid brother was an expert at putting his foot in it. Even in apologising he'd managed to point up his father's innate conservative nature.

"You know I don't often agree with our Phil, but I do think he's got a point, Dad. There's a lot happening in the farm machinery business these days, and it would be daft of us not to try to keep abreast of things."

Dan looked at him suspiciously. Jack usually didn't have much to say about farming. In fact, he suspected the lad wasn't cut out to be a farmer and several times he'd been on the verge of suggesting that he should consider finding something else to do. He couldn't fathom this new-found enthusiasm of Jack's.

"What changes have you got in mind, son?"

"I don't really know, but I was reading one of Philip's magazines the other day and it certainly made me think. They say it won't be long before there's a machine that won't only cut the cereals, it'll bundle and stack them as well, all in one operation. It seems to me it's only a matter of time before we can run the farm from some sort of control panel in the barn. We'll just press a series of buttons and the machines will get on with all the work."

Even Philip had the good grace to laugh. At first he'd thought Jack was genuinely on his side and he'd been pleasantly surprised. The sting in the tail didn't bother him. He knew he'd be proved right one day. Now that the war was over, he was convinced farming was on the move, and nothing could stop it.

CHAPTER FIVE

Bramble Cottage was just the latest in a long line of houses that Jack and Peggy had looked at. Like the others, it was all but derelict. The ad in the *Borchester Echo* had made it sound different somehow: "Idyllic, roses round the door . . . excellent possibilities." That should have warned them off. The cottage might be fit to live in one day, but one look at it told them it was going to take someone a great deal of time and a great deal of money. The Archers had little of either.

In one respect Bramble Cottage *was* different from most of the other places they'd seen so far. It did have a roof. And it *did* have roses – all over the place – but there wasn't a door. There was only an enormous crack all the way down the front of the brickwork from the roof to the top of the doorway – and that, presumably, was why the door had dropped off.

Jack put his arm round his wife's shoulders. He could tell she was even more disappointed than him.

"I'm sorry, old girl. We don't seem to be having much luck in this house-hunting lark."

Peggy could feel the tears starting in her eyes, but she was determined not to cry.

"Oh, Jack, what are we going to do? It's the last of the houses advertised in this week's paper. Do you think we'll ever find a place of our own around here? Maybe we should think about moving somewhere else and starting over again."

All he could do was nod in agreement. It didn't seem much to ask really – a few acres, room to keep a few sheep and two or three head of cattle, grow some potatoes and maybe one or two other vegetables. Peggy didn't want much either. He still remembered so clearly what she'd said when he'd asked her to marry him and move back to the village. She said she'd only come if she could have a little place with a garden full of giant hollyhocks and sweet williams, a tiny patch of grass where she could sit among the buttercups and daisies to listen to the bees humming and the birds singing. He'd felt a terrible wave of homesickness as she'd painted that picture of her ideal home – but then she'd made him laugh by demanding a compost patch as well where she could grow marrows and all the other vegetables she was going to need to build him up a bit!

Were all the disappointments making her change her mind – either about him or about living in the country?

"I know you're not happy, Peg, but let's give it a little longer before we decide on anything drastic."

"What do you mean by drastic?"

"Well, like going back to London. Don't forget I've got no qualifications so there won't be much of a job for me in the city, and if it's hard to find a place of our own here, I reckon it would be impossible in London."

She looked at him in surprise.

"What on earth would we want to go to London for? I couldn't wait to get away from all the noise and dirt. I'd dreamed of somebody like you coming along and whisking me away from all that! When I said we should think about moving somewhere else, I only meant somewhere else in the country."

"Like where, Peg?"

"Oh, I don't know . . . Devon, Cornwall . . . somewhere like that. Anywhere we can get a job and a house."

"Would you rather do that than stay on at Brookfield?"

In all the months they'd been staying at Brookfield, Doris and Dan had never made them feel anything less than at home, and Peggy had managed to buy one or two small pieces of furniture for their two rooms to give them a personal touch. When her mum had come up from London for a few weeks, Doris had really gone out of her way to make her comfortable and Mrs Perkins had vowed to come back to Ambridge and live there permanently one day – it was her idea of Paradise. No . . . Peggy had no complaints about living under her parents-in-law's roof. Eighteen months, however, was an awful long time to take advantage of anyone's kindness and Peggy was beginning to feel that she was exploiting Doris's good nature. How could she explain that to Jack?

"You know I'm very happy at Brookfield, Jack. That's got nothing to do with wanting to move. It's just that it seems as if we haven't started our married life together properly yet. We can't really build towards the future. Do you understand?"

Jack put his arms round her and hugged her.

"Aye, Peg, I understand all right. I just wanted to be sure that you weren't feeling you'd made a terrible mistake in marrying me."

"If you're searching for compliments, you're not going to get them, Jack Archer. I love you and I love little Jennifer and I wouldn't change either of you for the world . . . so please don't go all daft on me just because I say I'm fed up with looking at the umpteenth cottage and finding it's not fit to keep pigs in, let alone raise a family. Anybody would be fed up. Aren't you?"

"I'm sorry, love . . . of course I'm fed up. I can't go on working for Dad forever. I don't want to be a farmworker all my days. I want to be my own boss. But we've got to be realistic. Dad pays me a decent wage and we've got a roof over our heads with no likelihood of being turfed out if our face suddenly doesn't fit."

Jack had that trapped feeling again.

"I heard only the other day of a lad over at Loxley Barratt who was given his marching orders just because the farmer's son decided to get wed and wanted the poor beggar's cottage for himself. We don't want to find ourselves in that kind of situation do we?"

Peggy shook her head.

"You just wait until the government sorts itself out – that kind of thing won't be allowed any more. Clem Attlee's promised to look after folk like that."

"Aye, Peg, that's as may be, but I'm not too keen to wait for Mr Attlee to solve our problems for us."

Since the Labour Party's landslide victory the previous summer, Peggy seemed to keep expecting miracles. As far as Jack could see, they hadn't happened yet . . . certainly not in the vicinity of Ambridge.

"Come on, Peggy. Don't get going on one of your political lectures – we're not at Speakers' Corner now. What about a picnic? It's no good moping, and I've a feeling Mum put a whole basket of things in the back of the car for us!"

Knowing how much Peggy loved picnics, Jack hadn't had much difficulty that morning in persuading Doris to prepare a surprise meal for their house-hunting expedition. She'd urged him to make a day of it and had badgered Dan into lending Jack his car. Jack had planned the outing as a celebration, but now that their dream cottage had turned out to be a nightmare, he could only offer it as consolation.

Peggy hummed cheerfully to herself as she spread the white cloth on the grass and carefully set out the packets of sandwiches, the pickles and cheese and the homemade fruitcake that Doris Archer had packed away in the huge picnic basket. Her glumness had quite disappeared. Jack was relieved – he hated to see her unhappy.

While she fussed around, he picked up the *Borchester Echo* they'd brought with them and turned again to the small ads pages. He'd been through the "Farm Workpeople Wanted" column several times already and had followed up the few jobs advertised that offered accommodation, but he checked them again just to make sure he hadn't missed anything.

"Really reliable agricultural man wanted. Wages 70 shillings weekly with house and garden free."

That had turned out to be a waste of time because the job had gone before it even appeared in the paper, the farmer had said.

"£4 weekly for suitable man: indoor and outdoor jobs. Living accommodation available."

The living accommodation there had been a tiny attic room at the top of a scruffy old farmhouse. Peggy would never have survived climbing up and down all the stairs with the baby.

"General farmworker wanted, willing to help milk. Good lodgings near to work."

"Near" was two miles across the fields and the farmer wasn't interested when he discovered Jack was married.

The ad that had attracted him most was for "a farmhouse near village, to let to workman able to drive tractor. Knowledge of hops and fruits an advantage."

The farmer had seemed a nice enough chap to begin with and the job looked distinctly promising. But then the man had started making suggestions about how the rent could be so much cheaper and the wages ever so much higher "if the young lady had any time to spare a randy old man". Jack was not amused.

Having given up on the farm jobs, Jack looked next at the column advertising for "Clerks and Workpeople".

A barber and bath attendant was required at the Public Assistance Institute in Borchester. The wages were £3 10s a week plus an extra 19 shillings weekly war bonus. Jack wondered who the attendant had to bathe and barber. Probably every down-and-out in town.

Another vacancy caught his eye and made him think again about giving up farming and going into another job.

"Representative wanted to sell well-known veterinary medicines and to carry on the company's extensive connection among farmers in Borsetshire."

Jack was already seeing himself with a case of samples, but then his eye fell on the next line of the ad and he saw that "experience and own car" were necessary.

Suddenly he sat up.

"Look at this, Peg!"

"What is it?"

"It's an ad that's got into the wrong place, that's what . . . and it could be just what we're looking for."

Wedged among the "clerks and workpeople" was a two-line announcement.

"Smallholder has spare cottage to let. Some help useful."

The address was Low Road, Penny Hassett.

He hurried through the rest of the picnic, washing the last of Doris's baking down with a swift pint of ale. Then he packed Peggy and the basket back in the car and drove the short distance to Penny Hassett with growing excitement. He hoped nobody else had spotted the misplaced ad – perhaps this time he'd be the first to have a crack at it.

They stopped in Penny Hassett to ask a man the way to Low Road and were a bit taken aback by the curtness of his reply.

"You'll be looking for Frank Mead's place. Go across the common and turn right. Can't miss it."

He was right. Two little cottages stood fronting the road with about four or five acres of well-tended land between them. As the car stopped, a gaggle of geese burst into noisy alarm and that set the hens scattering in all directions.

Despite the warm summer afternoon, smoke was curling from the chimney of one of the cottages. They knocked at the door, and it was opened by a neatly dressed woman of about thirty-five who immediately introduced herself as Lizzie Mead.

"You'll have come about Frank's ad in the *Echo*."

It was more of a statement than a question and she didn't wait for an answer but disappeared into the house. A minute or so later, a man came to the door. He looked much older than his wife.

"I'm Frank Mead . . . please come in."

He ushered them into the front parlour where a fire was crackling merrily in the tiny grate.

"Sit down and let me have a look at you."

Peggy and Jack felt acutely uncomfortable beneath the man's piercing scrutiny. His sharp blue eyes peered hard into their faces. He seemed happy enough with what he saw in Peggy, but he appeared to recoil in horror from Jack.

"You've been drinking!"

Jack blinked in surprise.

"Well, yes . . . Peggy and I stopped to have a bit of a picnic and I washed it down with a glass of beer."

Frank Mead's eyes blazed.

"Alcohol is the Devil's weapon. It destroys men!"

Mrs Mead came into the room carrying a tray of tea. She looked slightly embarrassed.

"You must forgive Frank – he isn't feeling very well at the moment."

Jack gazed in astonishment as the man immediately slumped into an armchair and sat watching them in silence as his wife poured them some tea and offered them a slice of cake.

"Frank's worked very hard all his life and as you can see he's done a grand job around the farm . . ."

"Smallholding . . . it's not a farm . . . it's a smallholding. How often do I have to tell you?"

Frank Mead had suddenly become animated again and almost shouted at his wife. She didn't seem to mind.

"Yes, Frank, I'm sorry . . . the smallholding. Now please don't shout or you'll wake little Polly."

She turned back to Jack and Peggy.

"Sorry, as I was saying . . . he's done a grand job over the years but it's all beginning to get a bit too much for him and I'm not able to do too much myself because I've got a little girl – and I also have to spend more time with him now."

She almost whispered the last part of her sentence and looked guiltily across at her husband as if she'd betrayed his secret.

"We're looking for somebody who'll understand the situation and do whatever needs doing around the place. I won't pretend that it'll be an easy job but the other cottage is every bit as nice as this one and I'm sure it won't take you long to make yourselves very comfortable. If things go the way I expect, there's a very strong chance of the farm . . . sorry, smallholding . . . becoming available as well. Mind you, we'd have to come to some agreement about payment and things."

Jack and Peggy were stunned. They hadn't been in the house more than ten minutes and Mrs Mead seemed to be offering them the world on a plate.

"Maybe we could just look at the other cottage."

Jack sounded almost apologetic.

Before his wife could say anything, Frank Mead stood up.

"Just one moment. I'm still the master in this house. I'll conduct the negotiations if you don't mind, Lizzie."

The wildness had gone from his eyes and he spoke perfectly calmly. There was just a hint of a Borsetshire accent in his soft voice.

"You'll have to forgive my wife for appearing to rush things, Mr Archer. She's been very keen for me to take it a little easier for these past two years and she's anxious that I'm not going to change my mind as I did the last time we advertised."

Jack realised Peggy hadn't spoken a word since they'd knocked on the cottage door. She appeared completely dazed and watched in bemusement as Frank Mead opened the drawer of a sideboard and brought out a bible.

"I said a moment ago that alcohol was the Devil's weapon. I know, Mr Archer, I know. He has nearly destroyed me because of my weakness for drink. My health has gone and, as my wife will try to tell you if she thinks I can't hear her, my mind is going too. If you are to take over from me, I have to be sure that you don't share my frailty."

Jack shifted uncomfortably in his chair.

"Just a minute, Mr Mead. Peggy and I have only come to make preliminary enquiries. We were really more interested in the cottage. The ad didn't say anything about taking on the smallholding. It just said that you'd welcome some help."

Frank looked across at his wife and smiled at her.

"Lizzie is a very kind woman. She wouldn't want to hurt my feelings. She wouldn't want me to think she'd been trying to find someone to take my place. But that's the truth of the matter, Mr Archer. Now what we have to determine is whether or not you are the right man to follow me."

Jack glanced at Peggy and got quickly to his feet.

"I think we ought to be going now, Mr Mead. We need to be getting back to our little girl."

Frank Mead placed himself in front of Jack, almost blocking his way.

"Please don't go just yet. I want to make you an offer. Look around the smallholding – you'll find it in an excellent state. There are three pigs, two milk cows, three dozen hens – every one of them an excellent layer – and, as you may have noticed on the way in, an extremely noisy gaggle of geese. I've lifted all the potatoes, but there's plenty of space for a new planting and room for anything else you might want to grow. It's one of the best holdings in the whole of Borsetshire."

Jack had little doubt that he was right, but he knew there had to be a catch somewhere.

"I don't think I could afford to buy it, Mr Mead. I'd never be able to raise the price."

Frank Mead stared at him. His eyes were blazing again.

"The price is only your soul, young man. That's all."

He held the bible out towards Jack.

"All you have to do is place your hand on the bible. Renounce the Devil and the demon drink and you shall inherit my small world. Is that a price you can pay, Mr Archer?"

Jack took hold of Peggy's hand.

"It's something I'd have to think about, I'm afraid. I'll have to let you know!"

They hurried towards the door as Frank Mead slumped back into his chair. Mrs Mead followed them out.

"Please try to understand. Frank's not at all well. I can see you're honest young people so I would ask you not to mention this to anyone else. I'm frightened someone may come along and take advantage of his condition and leave me and my daughter penniless. You understand, don't you?"

It was Peggy who answered.

"Of course, we understand, but if I were you Mrs Mead, I'd have a word with a solicitor or somebody to protect yourself against your husband doing anything silly like giving away his property."

All the way back to Ambridge, Jack was very subdued. The incident had made him think about his own drinking habits. He didn't consider that he was a particularly heavy drinker but perhaps he was not the best person to judge. Alcoholics were supposed not to be able to admit their problem to themselves, or so he'd heard.

"Do you think I drink too much, Peggy?"

She laughed nervously.

"Yes, I do . . . but I don't think you're approaching poor Frank Mead's condition, if that's what you mean!"

That evening, for the first time in weeks, Jack didn't go down to The Bull. He stayed in and listened to the wireless.

Next day, he was out in the yard when Jim Price arrived with the morning post. It struck Jack that he might have come across a vacant house or property on his rounds.

"It's funny you should mention that now, but I've just been chatting to Amos Atkins. He's got a tenancy of about forty acres on the Manor Estate. Do you know it?"

"No, I can't say that I do."

"Only he was saying as how his Audrey hasn't been too well these past few months and the farm's been getting a bit run down. He thinks he might have to give it up but he's worried because he's got no one to pass it on to. It's not much of a place but the farmhouse is nice enough."

"Thanks Jim, it could be worth having a word with him."

"Aye, there's nothing to lose and I would guess the squire might be quite pleased to have another Archer as a tenant!"

Later that day Jack went off to see Amos Atkins. He received quite a rude shock when Amos didn't appear at all pleased to see him.

"You're not the sort that I'd want to recommend to the squire if I wanted to pass the tenancy on!"

Amos was nothing if not frank. Jack was taken aback because to the best of his knowledge they'd never spoken before, beyond a casual word in the pub of an evening.

"Why not, Mr Atkins?"

"They say as how you're a lazy beggar."

"Who says that?"

"Folk around the village. They say you've been taking Dan Archer for a ride. Got your wife and kid living off Brookfield they say."

Jack wasn't sure whether to be angry or upset.

"That's not fair!"

"There's no use bleating to me about it. I ain't saying it. I just know what I hear when I'm having my drink in the pub. And I knows you spends a lot of time in there . . . too much for a man that's supposed to be hard up and looking for a place of his own."

Jack shrugged his shoulders in resignation.

"It sounds as if you've made your mind up already without really knowing very much about me. It's true that when I came back to Ambridge, I couldn't get either a job or a place of my own, so we moved in to Brookfield. But my wife was expecting and we had nowhere else to go. What would you have done?"

Amos looked at him askance.

"Well, Jack Archer, I wouldn't have started from your position. I wouldn't have married a lass until I could give her what she deserved by way of a home and a bit of security, and I wouldn't have got her in the family way until I was good and ready to support a family. If you wants my opinion, I'd say you was an irresponsible young beggar. And if you wants to know what I'd say to the squire if he was to ask me about you taking over my farm . . . I'd say it would have to be over my dead body!"

Jack was shaken by the real venom in Amos Atkins' voice. He'd never stopped to consider what other people in the village might think about him. He hadn't really cared enough to give it much thought, but now he'd heard himself condemned out loud by a virtual stranger, he found it distressing.

He didn't say a word about what had occurred to Peggy when he got home, but he quietly resolved once again to turn over a new leaf. He was going to ease up on the drinking and he would work twice as hard. He was also more determined than ever to find a place of his own.

CHAPTER SIX

Peggy wasn't quite sure how to break it to Jack. He seemed to have so many worries already, and she couldn't bear the thought of adding to them. He needed her news like he needed a hole in the head. But there was no doubt about it. Dr Harvey had told her this morning that she was pregnant again.

She wasn't at all certain of her own feelings about it either. When she'd first suspected she might be having another baby, she'd been delighted. Then she'd started to count the cost of the extra burden it would put on their very meagre resources and much of her joy disappeared. She'd decided not to tell Jack about it straightaway in case it was a false alarm.

Her natural inclination was to confide in her mother-in-law. Doris Archer had so much experience of life and – yes – wisdom. She'd know best how to handle Jack. The trouble was that Jack would be furious if he ever got to know he wasn't the first to hear about the baby.

Living in his parents' home for so long had done nothing for his self-confidence. He'd become impossibly touchy. Peggy only had to mention some titbit she'd read in the paper or heard on the wireless to someone in the house other than Jack and he'd flare up immediately, then sulk for days. Doris didn't seem to take much notice, but Peggy could see that her father-in-law was losing patience with him. And she too was beginning to feel affected by Jack's moodiness.

Two years was much too long to spend under anybody else's roof. They really must get out. She was at the stage where she'd settle for almost anything. She'd even seriously thought about a tent after seeing one advertised for sale in the *Echo*!

Reading the paper was one of Peggy's great pleasures. There were few books at Brookfield and Jack didn't have a single one to his name. He said farming

71

folk never had time to read. Certainly, since young Philip had gone off to the Farming Institute, no one in the house seemed to do much reading. She couldn't afford to buy any books of her own, and since she'd had Jennifer, she didn't often get the chance to go to the library.

So she had to make do with the *Borchester Echo* and she found it an endless source of information and entertainment. Every week she scoured it from cover to cover. It was through the *Echo* she knew how to cure almost every ailment known to mankind. Suffering from backache? Try Doan's Kidney Backache Pills . . . and there was Pineate Honey Syrup to clear clogged-up passages . . . Beecham's Powders for flu . . . Fynnon Salts for rheumatism . . . even Menopax to relieve the symptoms of the menopause! Peggy sometimes felt she could have taken a degree in medicine.

She also read about all the dances and social functions throughout the county, and she would dream of waltzing and twirling in a new frock to the music of Harold Rich or Victor Silvester, especially when she'd been listening to him on the wireless.

Like Jack, she pored over the "Accommodation to Let" column and the job advertisements. However, after two years of constant hope giving way to disappointment, even Peggy's natural enthusiasm was getting eroded. Sometimes she thought it might be Jack's fault for not trying hard enough . . . like the time they'd heard about a place in Loxley Barratt, and he'd been two hours late to see the landlord's agent because he'd stopped off at The Bull and forgotten about the appointment.

Now with Jennifer off her hands for a couple of hours – Jack had taken her for a walk up on Lakey Hill – she had a chance to go through this week's paper yet again. She'd already been through it with a fine-tooth comb, hoping against hope there'd be something there to tell Jack about . . . something to take his mind off the news she was going to have to break to him sooner or later.

There was nothing.

As she scanned the columns for the umpteenth time, her mother-in-law came into the kitchen.

"Aren't you going to the WI today, Peg?"

Peggy looked at the clock and jumped up.

"Gosh, I didn't realise it was that late. Yes, I am going. Aren't you?"

"No, I've got too much on at the moment. I'll have to give it a miss. Will you give my apologies?"

Peggy felt guilty. She loved the weekly meeting of the Women's Institute. It was a chance to meet the other women in the village, and she was fascinated by some of the speakers the committee managed to persuade to come along. But if Doris was too busy to go, Peggy ought to offer to help her out. Her better nature got the better of her.

"I'm not particularly bothered about going to the meeting so if there's anything you want me to do, I'll willingly lend a hand, Mum."

Doris looked at her and smiled.

"No, there's nothing you can do, thank you. You go along and enjoy yourself while you can!"

"Whatever do you mean?"

"Well . . . if I'm not very much mistaken, it will only be another two or three months before you're in no condition to get down to the village hall."

Peggy blushed.

"But how did you guess?"

"Intuition!"

"Oh, Mum, you won't say anything to Jack will you? I haven't told him yet and you know what he's like. If he thinks he's not the first to know, he'll go all peculiar on me."

"Whyever haven't you told him yet, Peg? You must have known a good week or two by now."

"To be honest, I did have a pretty shrewd idea, but Dr Harvey didn't confirm it until this morning. I haven't told Jack yet because I don't think this is the right time. He seems so fed up at the moment that I thought it would be better to wait and see if anything came up this week that might cheer him up a bit."

It was Doris's turn to feel guilty. Her Jack was being a pain in the neck and wasn't playing fair by Peggy. She couldn't understand him. He was never really happy for any length of time these days. In fact he'd not been right since he'd been in the army. He'd always been just a bit too keen on drinking to Doris's way of thinking, but now it seemed he'd also taken to gambling quite heavily. It was Dan who had told her about his betting on the horses, but they both reckoned Peggy knew nothing about it. Doris wasn't planning to tell her . . . and especially not now when she was worried about having an extra mouth to feed.

"You'd better hurry or you'll miss the meeting, Peg. We'll have a chat about things some other time and, of course, I won't say a word to Jack."

By the time she reached the hall the meeting had already started. A plump, emphatic woman was telling the assembled women how to cure bacon. Peggy wasn't very interested. Doris had already taught her to do all that.

The talk over, Peggy mingled with the other women, enjoying all the chatter that went on over the cups of tea. She was the youngest member of the Institute and she always found everyone ready to pass on titbits of advice or else there was some new piece of gossip, or some story from Ambridge's past to absorb. She'd discovered a lot about the village since she started coming to the WI sessions.

One story she was convinced was a load of bunkum concerned the ghost of a little drummer boy from the Civil War who was supposed to haunt The Bull. Peggy was certain any strange noises the regulars claimed to have heard had more to do with the amount of alcohol they'd consumed than anything else. She hadn't asked Jack about it though – she was afraid he'd almost certainly have been one of those who'd claimed to have heard the ghostly drum-beats!

Peggy asked Betty Barrett if she'd missed anything interesting at the beginning of the meeting.

"Depends on what you call interesting, my dear. If you fancy learning to make gloves, there's a two-day refresher course in Felpersham next month!"

Peggy giggled.

"There won't be too many from Ambridge going to that, will there?"

"I didn't notice too many hands going up, I must say. The only other thing is this new country club at Felpersham. The premises are now open, it seems, and the annual subscription is five shillings a year. They're going to start serving light luncheons and afternoon teas sometime next month. It could be quite handy if you do your shopping over there."

Peggy would have loved to join but she knew there wasn't any point. There was no way she could get to Felpersham without scrounging a lift, and she didn't like doing that too often. She'd suggested to Jack that she ought to have a bike and he'd thought it was a good idea until he realised the cheapest one would cost somewhere between seven and eight pounds. Then he wasn't so keen. He hadn't said that was the reason though. His excuse was that there was so much traffic on the road that cycling wasn't safe any more.

"Are you a member, Mrs Barrett?"

"No, not at the moment but I'm going to have a word with Fred about it and see what he says. Oh, by the way, have you and young Jack been able to find anywhere to live yet?"

Peggy shook her head wearily. Mrs Barrett must have asked her the same question at every meeting for the past year.

"As a matter of fact, the reason I was late was because I was looking through the paper to see if anything had come up this week. No luck, I'm afraid."

Mrs Barrett leaned over to whisper confidentially in Peggy's ear.

"Have you heard about Amos Atkins? You know he's been talking about giving up?"

Peggy was disappointed. She'd thought for a wonderful moment Betty Barrett was going to offer a new piece of information about a vacant house.

"Yes, I'm afraid so. We've already tried him. Jack went to see him some months ago but although he hadn't finally made up his mind, we got the impression he was pretty sure he was going to carry on."

Mrs Barrett nodded enthusiastically.

"But that's exactly the point. Audrey's been much better of late and they've now finally decided to carry on for another few years at least, and that means Rickyard Cottage will be available!"

Peggy couldn't believe her ears. Rickyard Cottage was only a spit away from Brookfield and she'd dreamed about being able to rent it from the day she first set eyes on it. There hadn't seemed much likelihood of that because it was occupied by Sam Peters, one of the estate cowmen, and he and his wife Alice didn't seem to want to move. That it might now be available was too good to be true.

"But what has the Atkins' decision got to do with Rickyard Cottage?"

It was a complicated story.

"Sam Peters has been after a tenancy for several years now and the squire had more or less promised him the next one that came up. When Amos started talking about packing up, the squire suggested that he do a swap with Sam . . . take over Rickyard Cottage and develop the few acres around it as a bit of a smallholding if he felt like it. Everybody seemed to be happy with the idea, especially Sam and Alice."

Peggy could understand exactly how they felt.

"They must have been very disappointed when Amos changed his mind."

"I don't think disappointed is the word. Sam was livid, but there was nothing the squire could do about it. Amos can hang on to the tenancy as long as he likes and, in any case, I couldn't see the squire wanting to turf him out. He's had to offer Sam a better job and a better house to go with it. Sam and Alice are moving closer to the estate office in a month or so."

"And you reckon that will leave Rickyard Cottage empty? Isn't there a queue of people waiting for it?"

"Oh, I don't know what the score is about the letting, Peggy. Your Jack ought to go and see the squire pretty quickly, though."

Peggy could hardly wait to get away from the meeting. She sped through the farewells and rushed back to Brookfield. To her annoyance, Jack had been back and left Jennifer with Doris before going off again.

"Have you no idea where he went?"

She realised she sounded impatient with Doris and immediately apologised.

"That's all right, Peg. You don't need to worry about things like that with me. Have you decided now's the time to tell Jack about the new baby?"

Peggy felt trapped again. She'd actually forgotten about the baby, but she didn't want to confide her latest piece of news to her mother-in-law and risk making Jack cross.

He, for once, chose exactly the right moment to return. He came clattering into the kitchen in a cheerful enough mood and seemed pleased, though surprised, when Peggy threw her arms round him.

"Oh, Jack, I've got some terrific news."

Doris Archer smiled and went upstairs to sort through the linen cupboard. Jack looked at his wife warily.

"What is it, Peg? You're not pregnant again, are you?"

Peggy was stunned. What could she say? She'd been rehearsing how to tell him about Rickyard Cottage without letting him think she'd been making enquiries behind his back. She decided to go for broke.

"What's the plural of news?"

She could see the puzzlement in his eyes.

"What I mean, Jack, is that I've got two pieces of terrific news. You've guessed the first one!"

He did his best to look pleased.

"Gosh, Peg, that's smashing. I'm thrilled."

"Wait until you hear the other piece . . . Rickyard Cottage is available for rent!"

If she'd bashed him on the head, he couldn't have looked more bemused.

"Available? What do you mean, available? The Peters live there. In fact I was talking to Sam about ten minutes ago. I came past Rickyard Cottage on my way home. He didn't say anything to me about moving."

Peggy sat him down and patiently explained Betty Barrett's story as quickly as she could.

"Now all you have to do is go and see the squire."

"See the squire? I can't do that. I can't just bowl up and demand to see the squire because I think a cottage *might* be available. What do you want me to say? My wife was gossiping at the WI and someone said they thought etc etc . . . I'd get thrown out on my ear. The squire's a very busy man, you know."

Peggy felt like crying. A golden opportunity had fallen into their laps and Jack was making excuses not to pick it up. He was too scared to go to the squire. Or was there more to it than that? Was he actually too scared to cut himself free from Brookfield? Had all the disappointments of the past two years just been feigned? Did he really prefer to stay put? She couldn't believe that.

"I don't mind going to see the squire myself, Jack. Or we can go together, whichever you prefer. But we have to do it right now before it's too late. If we lose this opportunity, I'll never forgive myself."

What she wanted to say was she'd never forgive him. She didn't have to. He understood.

"I'll ask Dad if I can borrow the car."

While Jack was away, Peggy explained the situation to Dan and Doris. They were thrilled. Dan was more excited about the new baby than about Rickyard Cottage.

"It's really grand news, lass. Do you think maybe it'll be a boy this time?"

Doris looked at him crossly.

"Don't you start pressuring the girl, Dan Archer. It's not up to her whether it'll be a boy or girl. I know you want a grandson, but you'll just have to wait until one comes along. There's no use whistling like you do with your dog, you know."

Peggy could hardly attend to their pleased comments and kept looking impatiently out of the window to see if Jack was back.

"What do you think the squire will say, Dad? Do you think he'll let us have the cottage?"

Dan rubbed his chin thoughtfully.

"I'm not rightly sure, lass. If it was just the cottage, I'm sure he'd agree without too much fuss. But if you say the plan is to develop a smallholding as well, that's a different matter. He won't hand out a tenancy as easy as that, I'm afraid. He'll want to know all about Jack's plans and not just for the next few years, but in the long term as well. He'll need an awful lot more information than you and Jack are likely to be able to give him off the top of your heads."

He was right. Jack came back looking very glum.

"It's not very hopeful, I'm afraid, Peggy. The squire's agent says the . . ."

"The squire's agent? You mean you didn't even get to see Mr Lawson-Hope himself?"

Jack looked sheepish.

"He wasn't in his office at the time."

Peggy was exasperated.

"Oh, never mind. What did his agent say?"

"He says the cottage is going to be vacant right enough, but it goes with the adjacent land and that'll have to be developed into a smallholding."

Peggy could hardly contain herself.

"But that's perfect. It's exactly what we've been looking for! If there's no smallholding there now, think of the fun we can have planning and developing it for ourselves."

"Slow down, Peg. It's not for us, I'm afraid. The agent says the squire's looking for someone with a lot more experience than I've got. He was expecting Amos Atkins to take it on. It's not very likely that he'll let it go to us."

Peggy looked at him with a rare scowl on her face.

"Now just you wait a minute, Jack Archer. Is this place available or not?"

"Aye, it's available."

"And did the squire's agent say categorically that he wouldn't let you and me have a go at it?"

"Well . . . not exactly."

"Stop hedging. Did he say he wouldn't consider us as tenants?"

"No, he didn't say that, but then he didn't say that he would either."

Peggy was angry now, and for the first time in her married life, she let it show.

"Damn it, Jack. You're accepting defeat without even putting up a fight. If the squire's agent, let alone the squire himself, didn't say we had no chance of becoming the tenants then in my book that means we've got as good a chance as anybody else. What do you think, Dad?"

Dan and Doris had been sitting listening to the exchanges in silence. Doris had seen odd flashes of Peggy's temper before, but it came as a complete revelation to Dan. His admiration for her went up even higher.

"I think, Peg, that if our Jack shows half the spirit you do, he'll have the squire eating out of his hand and begging to get a tenancy agreement thrashed out afore next Lady Day!"

Everyone laughed and the tension was broken. Peggy hugged Jack and he did his best to regain control of the situation, but her flash of temper had made it clear to everyone there, not least to Jack himself, that their marriage was now very much a partnership of equals . . . at least. Peggy wasn't for pushing around.

When Jack went to see the squire again two days later, Peggy was with him. The squire asked lots of awkward questions, but with Dan's help they'd done their homework beforehand. They managed to answer most of them. Whether or not their answers were to his satisfaction was another matter. He didn't give any indication either way.

They only realised the interview was over when the squire quite suddenly stood up.

"Well, goodbye. Thank you for coming to see me, Jack. It's been very nice to meet you, Mrs Archer. If you don't mind me saying so, you remind me very much of your mother-in-law."

"Why, thank you Mr Lawson-Hope. That's a very nice compliment."

"Yes . . . I remember how enthusiastically she took to life on the farm and I'm sure Dan Archer would be the first to admit she's played a very important part in helping to build up Brookfield Farm. I'm sure you'll do the same at Rickyard. You're a very lucky man, Jack. I wish you both good luck in your new venture."

Peggy was frightened to say anything in case she'd misunderstood. Had the squire actually said they were to be the new tenants of Rickyard Cottage *and* smallholding? He was certainly shaking Jack's hand heartily enough.

Outside, all her doubts were swept away. Jack gave her an enormous bear hug.

"Well, you've done it, girl. You've got us the new start in life we've been looking for. We're going to be farmers . . . well, smallholders. Mr and Mrs Jack

Archer of Rickyard Cottage . . . no, Mr Jack Archer and his wife, Peggy Archer! Doesn't it sound grand?"

She said nothing. She couldn't. The tears were rolling down her cheeks. They were tears of happiness. She was speechless with joy.

Dan and Doris came out into the yard with little Jennifer when they drove up in the car. Nobody needed to ask any questions and nobody had to say anything. The look on Peggy's face said everything.

When she'd eventually put Jennifer to bed, Peggy came back downstairs and got out the *Borchester Echo*. She'd a new home to plan and she knew exactly where to start.

"Have a look at this, Jack!"

It was the page with the furniture advertisements.

Jack had more to worry about than how to furnish the cottage. There were a million and one things that would have to be arranged before he could get the smallholding under way, but he knew there was no point in arguing with Peggy. He did as he was told. He looked at the furniture ads. There were dozens of them, but Peggy was only interested in one.

"Fine furniture – just what you want at just the prices you can afford. Visit our showrooms where a friendly welcome awaits you. All the latest new designs in figured walnut and oak bedroom suites . . . from £49 19s 6d (or by extended payments of 45 shillings monthly); carved oak and burr walnut dining-room suites . . . from £33 19s 6d (or monthly payments of 30 shillings); lounge suites at MOST reasonable prices . . . from £28 17s 6d (monthly payments 25 shillings). Everything for the happy home."

Peggy had looked at this same advertisement almost every week for the last two years. She'd planned every stick of furniture she would need for her new house. It didn't matter how many rooms it had, or what shape or size they were. She'd planned for every conceivable combination. She knew where the oak bedroom suite would go . . . she didn't like figured walnut. She could see the carved oak dining suite in a cosy little separate dining room, and she'd already decided on the colour of the lounge suite and the curtains she'd need to make to match it. She'd be happy to make do with linoleum at first, though. Carpets could come later.

Rickyard Cottage was as good as furnished. All that was needed was for John Lunn Ltd to deliver the goods, and that would be fairly easy . . . now that they had the address.

CHAPTER SEVEN

Courage had come late to Jack Archer. For years he had always taken the easy way out of difficult situations. The only other time in his life that he'd had the chance to show what he was really made of, he'd been thwarted by a wheezy chest and an over-zealous MO. Now there'd been no excuses, no doctor to stand behind – no one, in fact, to hold him back from proving the raw courage he had always believed was inside him.

For it had taken courage of a special kind to take on the nine acres of derelict land that went with Rickyard Cottage – land which had never been cultivated for as far back as anyone in the village could remember, and was overgrown with coarse grass, nettles, dockleaves, thistles and every other kind of weed. Behind high, unkempt hedges was the debris of years of wilful neglect – discarded farm implements, broken furniture, tin baths, old bikes and an astonishing collection of household rubbish.

Sam Peters had never had the time or the inclination to do anything with the land. It wasn't his. He'd never been asked to look after it, and he had never felt any responsibility for it. It had just been there. All this, Jack Archer had undertaken to change when he had signed his tenancy agreement with the squire. It was a task that demanded blood and sweat and tears and toil, as Jack had remarked to Peggy, in full-throated Churchillian tones, as they contemplated the work before them.

The blood had come from the broken blisters on his hands after hours of struggling to keep the plough turning the frost-hardened ground. The sweat had flowed freely as he'd knuckled down to sixteen or seventeen hours hard labour a day, working like a man possessed – determined to do better than anyone expected of him, to show his wife that he had the will to succeed, to prove to his father that there was another farmer in the Archer family. The tears had come at night when the muscles in his aching limbs were seized and knotted with cramp and Peggy had rubbed the tension from them. There'd been secret tears at other times, too, but he didn't talk about them to anyone.

The toil had been endless and back-breaking. His first job had been to clear all the debris from the fields. Whole cartloads of rubbish had to be shifted before he could begin to cut down the tall grass and overgrown weeds. That had meant working solidly for three months all over Christmas because he was determined to start turning over the soil on Plough Monday, the first Monday after Twelfth Night and the traditional start to the farmer's year. It had been touch and go, though, and as the day loomed nearer it assumed more and more symbolic importance for Jack.

He might never have made it at all if it hadn't been for George Grundy. He'd had very little experience of using a scythe and having no idea of how to set about cutting the long grass that had fallen over and been flattened by the wind and rain, he was making agonisingly slow progress. He could have wept with frustration – it looked as if it would be Easter at least before he was ready for ploughing if he went on at this rate. A little reluctantly, because he hated asking for help, he'd mentioned his problems in The Bull one night. George hadn't said anything at the time, but the next day he was knocking on the door of Rickyard Cottage with a newly sharpened scythe over his shoulder. He'd come not to offer advice, but to help do the job.

George enjoyed using the scythe. He found great satisfaction in the regular swishing sound of the blade as it cut through the grass, and he enjoyed the rhythmic swing of the finely balanced implement as he hacked through even the thickest of the weeds and brambles. And although he would never have said it out loud, he found it even more satisfying to be needed by Dan Archer's boy. He revelled in the irony of offering advice and help to Jack – that was one in the eye for Daniel-high-and-mighty-Archer. There'd always been rivalry between the two men since they'd been opponents in the village ploughing matches back in the old days just after the First War.

Perhaps shamed by George Grundy's lead, several other neighbours dropped in after that to offer the odd bit of help or the occasional word of advice and Jack enjoyed the feeling of comradeship and acceptance by his fellow farmers. It made him feel good. It made Peggy feel good too. Jack was much happier and more amenable these days than she'd ever known him.

Peggy, too, was happy . . . now.

She'd been shocked when she first saw the inside of Rickyard Cottage. With its neat coat of whitewash and Alice Peters' freshly laundered curtains at the windows, it had always seemed very attractive from the outside, especially in the summer sunlight. She'd cast many a longing glance at it when she'd passed it.

Inside, though, it was a very different story, as she soon found out. The walls of the small living-room were smoke-blackened and it didn't take Peggy long to find out why. Anxious to make the place seem more cheerful, she'd hurried to light a fire in the tiny grate, and immediately the room was filled with billowing smoke that threatened to suffocate her and little Jennifer. The chimney was blocked by several birds' nests which Peggy had to dislodge with a long branch before she dared get a fire going again.

The kitchen had been a revelation. There were no proper cooking facilities, simply a small fireplace with two swivel hobs that could be pushed over the flames. There was one tiny sink, but the drainpipe wasn't connected to anything and the waste ran into a bucket which had to be emptied almost every five minutes. Instead of a larder, there was only a narrow cold shelf just inside the back door, so low that any passing cat or dog was in easy reach of whatever dainty morsel anyone might have been daft enough to place there.

As if all this was not bad enough, Peggy had been horrified to see the gas bracket still covered with a chipped glass shade and a blackened gas mantle. However, the cottage also had a rudimentary electric generator which gave a flickering and uncertain supply, and it all seemed a little like something out of the Dark Ages to Peggy.

Never one to let things get her down for long, Peggy had been delighted by the way her friends had rallied round to help. She'd had offers of curtains and bits of furniture from all over the village and Betty Barrett called regularly to lend a hand with the scrubbing and cleaning.

Prue Harris – one of the few girls in the village around Peggy's age – was also a regular caller. She often brought a picnic basket with her to give Peggy a break and a bite to eat without having to worry about cooking on the ancient hobs. It was a lovely gesture and Peggy couldn't understand why Jack always refused to join them. She couldn't help noticing that he always seemed slightly jumpy when Prue was around and it crossed her mind to wonder if it had anything to do with Prue's being an occasional barmaid at The Bull.

It did. Jack had run up a fairly hefty slate in the pub and he was on tenterhooks that Prue might mention it to Peggy. He didn't want her to know just how hard up they were. Jack always found time to nip down to The Bull for a quick drink no matter how busy he was and no matter how hard he'd been working. Peggy didn't mind. She thought he'd earned the break. She didn't even mind when he rolled home slightly the worse for wear. At least he was always cheerful these days – not like the old truculence when he'd had too much to drink.

These were the most satisfying days of Jack's life. On Plough Monday in 1947 – a date circled in red on the calendar in the kitchen at Rickyard Cottage – he was ready with a borrowed horse and newly bought plough to start turning over his own land. He had proved

Amos Atkins, and all the others that had doubted him, wrong. Indeed, they had looked on in admiration as he'd worked tirelessly through October and November and December to perform the near miracle of turning his derelict acres into the beginnings of an efficient smallholding. Perhaps Jack Archer was going to be as good a farmer as his father after all.

In January, his courage was tested as it had never been before. The country suffered the worst winter in living memory. Only days after Plough Monday it had begun to snow, and then it continued to snow for seven weeks. For three weeks at a stretch, the temperature never rose above zero.

Factories were closed down and nearly three million people were thrown out of work. Fuel supplies ran short and housewives had to cope without electricity for long periods every day. The BBC's new television service was abandoned, the Third Programme was shut down and both the Light Programme and the Home Service were curtailed at eleven o'clock each evening.

In the countryside, the snow was so deep that nothing stirred. Thousands of sheep were cut off and perished without feedstuffs. In the Cotswolds, two motorists died after being trapped in their cars under the drifting snow. Miles of electricity supply lines and telephone wires were brought down under the weight of snow and large parts of the country were blacked out.

Jack had managed to get all his 45 sheep, his three milk cows, six goats and four pigs safely into the old barn and the yard behind the cottage, and he was able to keep them well fed and reasonably warm. Unable to get out into the fields, he had regularly cleared the snow from around Rickyard Cottage and when he'd done that he'd paced up and down, anxious and frustrated at not being able to get on with his work. He'd whiled away his time by chopping more firewood than he and Peggy would have been able to burn in a month of Sundays. He was terrified of losing the pace and rhythm of his labours.

Now, in early March, it was slowly beginning to thaw and the sludgy colours of winter were at last giving way to the brave new greens of springtime growth. But then the wireless weather forecasts were warning of a new menace – torrential rain.

Already other parts of the country had been very badly hit. In Scotland, eleven inches of rain had fallen in one 48-hour period. Rivers, already swollen by the thawing snow and ice, burst their banks and in the North of England several towns had been badly flooded. The forecasts said the rain was heading towards the Midlands and would arrive on the Sunday or Monday.

On Sunday morning, Jack and Peggy heard it pattering against the bedroom window and decided to have a long lie-in. This was a rare luxury for them, and they lay there happily listening to Sandy Macpherson on the BBC organ. As he finished his recital of favourite hymn tunes, yet another weather forecast came on the air. It seemed to drone on and on for ever and Peggy drifted away, not really listening. Suddenly she felt Jack go tense beside her.

"What's the matter, love?"

"Didn't you hear the man? He said more than five inches of rain have fallen in the West Midlands overnight – the worst in memory. I've just remembered, Peg – I haven't cut any drainage ditches!"

"What does that mean?"

Jack was halfway out of the room, pulling on his trousers and hopping on one foot as he tugged a sock and boot on the other.

"It means we could lose everything if I don't get out there sharpish and do something about it fast! Do you think you could nip up to Brookfield and tell Dad what's wrong and ask if there's any help he can give me."

Outside, it was clear that Jack had heeded the forecasters' warnings too late. He could see that the ground was already waterlogged and the rain was still coming down in stair-rods. Water was pouring down the slope from Heydon Brook and was beginning to collect in large pools on his fields.

Not bothering with oilskins, he grabbed a spade and ran across the field as fast as the greasy surface would let him. Twice he fell headlong and by the time he'd reached the farthest edge of his land, he could taste the mud in his mouth and feel it even in his ears. As he feverishly started digging a trench, the rain lashed at him and he found it difficult to stay upright. At least the ground was soft and the sharp spade sliced through it quickly and easily.

Twenty minutes later two figures shrouded in oilskins came across the field to join him. It was his father and Ned Larkin. He'd only managed to dig a couple of feet or so of ditch.

"It be a bit late to start a-diggin' this ditch now, Master Jack. You should a done it afore now."

Jack didn't have the breath to waste on saying what he felt.

His father took one look at his bedraggled state and put his hand on his shoulder to stop him.

"It's pointless, Jack. There's nothing we can do now. It would take two days to dig a proper trench in normal conditions. It'll take forever in this weather. Anyway, it's too late for ditches as Ned says."

Jack shrugged off the hand and started digging in an even greater frenzy.

"If you don't want to help then clear off. I'm not going to stand by and watch months of work disappear just like that."

His words came out in great gasps and the wheeze in his chest was almost as loud as the wind slicing across the waterlogged fields. His father regarded him anxiously.

"For God's sake, Jack, listen to me. You go back and get proper togged out for this sort of job and Ned and me will have a go at getting some sort of drain going. You're going at it all the wrong way. You'll have to go further up the slope for a start."

"I don't care about further up the slope, that's not my land. This is my land right here!"

"Aye, lad, I know all that, but if you don't give the water a pathway up there it'll be straight onto your land in no time. You can see how bad it is already."

The pools of water were getting bigger all the time and two fields were already totally submerged in several inches. Jack refused to take any notice and went on digging where he was. Dan shook his head and turned to Ned.

"You go back and see if you can raise Jess Allard and his lads. See if they'll bring over their new tractor and we can try hitching up a plough and getting it across the slope there."

Ned hurried away and Dan turned again to his son.

"Come on, lad. Pack it in. Leave it until the tractor gets here. See some sense. You'll get your death of cold out here."

Jack was beyond feeling the cold or the wet.

"I don't care about the cold, Dad. I can't just stand and do nothing. I've got to have a go."

"You're not achieving anything. Leave it and we'll have a go when the tractor comes. Another half-hour's not going to make any difference, except to your health."

"Damn my health!"

Dan grabbed him angrily by the shoulder.

"You can't say that any more, Jack lad. It's not just your own skin you've got to worry about. You've got a lot more responsibilities now. There's Peg and Jennifer and the new baby on the way. Think about them. What'll they do if you go sick on them? You're no use to them laid up in a sick bed for months."

He was wasting his breath. Nothing would drag Jack away from his precious land. It was as if his whole life was running away before his very eyes. He hacked at the ground with his spade and dragged out chunks of mud with his bare hands. The rain was slashing down so heavily it had torn the shirt half off his back and he'd lost both his boots in the mud. His attempts at digging a ditch were about as effective as trying to catch water in a paper bag.

Unable to stop him any other way, Dan again grabbed his son by the shoulder and swung him round to face him . . . only this time he hit him on the chin with the heaviest punch he could swing. There was a terrible crack as his fist connected. Jack looked at him in amazement and then his eyes glazed over and he slumped to the ground.

With the rain beating down on him, Dan Archer looked at the limp body on the ground and remembered the last time he'd struck such a blow. That time it had been his younger brother Ben he'd laid low. The following day Ben had disappeared and was next heard of in Canada. Dan prayed nothing so disastrous would happen this time. When Jack came to, he hoped he'd understand Dan had struck him for his own good. As he struggled to pick his son up, Peggy came plodding and floundering across the quagmire of mud. A look of fear spread across her face when she saw Jack lying flat out.

"My God, what's happened, Dad? What's the matter with Jack? Is he all right?"

She was nearly hysterical with fear.

"He's all right, Peg. He's just had a bit of an accident. Nothing serious. He'll be fine when we get him back to the house. Can you just give me a hand to get him over my shoulder?"

Peggy leaned down to look into Jack's ashen face and then stretched to help Dan get his hands under the inert body. As she did, she let out a yell of pain and collapsed in the squelching mud, sprawling alongside her husband.

Dan looked at her in dismay. He'd forgotten for a moment that she was pregnant. She lay there gasping for breath and in obvious agony.

"Just hang on a second, love. I'll cover our Jack and then I'll get you back to the cottage as quickly as I can!"

"No, don't worry about me, Dad. I'll be all right. Look after Jack. He'll get pneumonia or worse."

Dan stripped off his own oilskins and covered Jack as best he could, though there seemed little point as he was already soaked to the skin.

"Right, now Peg, no arguments. We'll get you into the warm and I'll come straight back for Jack."

Before she could argue any further, he lifted her up and started the long slippery walk across the field, afraid to hurry for fear of losing his footing. The rain lashed at both of them and Peggy tried her best to spread her cape over him, but to little effect.

"Please leave me, Dad. I'll be fine. Please go and help Jack."

Dan was too breathless to speak. He just shook his head and struggled on towards the cottage. Peggy tried to wriggle free, but as she did she was wracked by another great spasm of pain. She let out a terrible groan and Dan carried her half-fainting the rest of the way.

The door to the cottage was off the latch and banging in the wind. Dan pushed it open and was horrified by the chaos that confronted him. It looked as if the storm had blown straight through the kitchen. A milk churn had overturned and poured its contents over half the floor. A basket of eggs had somehow been toppled from the table and the broken shells ground underneath his feet. Upstairs he could hear Jennifer crying in her cot.

He pushed his way past an upturned chair into the front parlour and put Peggy gently down on the settee. She looked terrible. Her face was contorted with pain and she was covered from head to toe with mud. He eased off her oilskin cape and saw that it had been scant protection against the rain. She was soaked through to the skin. He looked around, but there was nothing in the room to use to cover her up.

He thought about Jack still lying where he'd left him, in the torrential rain. Just then, Peggy let out another moan and another spasm wracked her body. He ran upstairs and pulled the blankets off the bed. When he got back, Peggy was curled up like a ball and was shivering from head to foot. For once in his life, Dan Archer didn't know what to do. She clearly needed a doctor urgently, but there was still Jack to attend to. Why had he raised his fist to him? Surely he could have brought him to his senses some other way?

Quickly Dan made up his mind. Peggy and the baby had to come first. As fast as his frozen fingers would let him, he stripped off Peggy's wet clothes and wrapped her in a blanket. He rubbed her all over through the blanket and then took it off and replaced it with another one.

He looked at her closely. It was difficult to tell through the streaks of mud, but he thought there was a little colour coming back to her cheeks. She stirred and looked up at him.

"Jack? How's Jack?"

"Never mind Jack for the moment, love. Do you feel all right? I'll get the doctor to you in a minute."

"Where's Jack? I want Jack. Please get me Jack. Oh, Dad, what's happening? Is Jack all right?"

Dan looked at her guiltily.

"Will you be all right on your own for a few minutes while I go and help Jack? I'll get him to come back inside now."

There was no point telling her the truth at this stage.

As he struggled back through the rain and across the field, he saw that Jack had managed to pull himself up into a sitting position. When he reached him, he could see he was still very dazed.

"Are you all right, lad?"

The only answer was a slight nod of the head.

Dan tried to lever him up but the mud made it very difficult and he kept having to readjust his grip. Eventually he got his son's limp body over his shoulder in a fireman's lift and started the long trudge back to the house. Halfway across, Ned Larkin and

Jess Allard arrived on a small tractor. They jumped out and took Jack from him. Dan was happy to let them take over.

"As soon as you've got him back to the house, you take the tractor Jess and fetch Dr Harvey quick. Peg's taken bad in there and get some womenfolk – they'll be needed all right!"

Within minutes, it seemed, help had arrived from all sides. By the time Dan had got Jack upstairs and the wet clothes off him, Dr Harvey and Doris were in the parlour tending to Peggy and Mabel Larkin and Jeannie Allard were trying to sort out the debris in the kitchen. Young Christine was trying to make a pot of tea but was having difficulty in finding where everything was.

Dan suddenly felt exhausted and started to shiver with the cold. Young Christine, trying not to cry, thrust a cup of steaming hot tea into his hand.

"I hope it's all right, Dad. I've put some whisky in it. That's what Dr Harvey told me to do. He gave me the whisky."

Slumped in the wooden armchair by the kitchen fire, Dan smiled.

"That's just grand, Christine, just grand."

Jeannie Allard started fussing around him, but he was recovering fast.

"Don't you worry about me, Jeannie. When I've drunk this tea, I'll go back to Brookfield and sort myself out with some dry clothes. I'll be as right as rain . . . heck, I shouldn't say that should I? I'll be fine in no time at all."

Jeannie shrugged her countrywoman's shoulders. She was used to strong men.

"Just as you please, Dan Archer, but I'm here to help if I'm needed."

"Thanks, Jeannie, it's very good of you. How's young Peg?"

"The doctor's still with her."

Dan nodded. It was quite clear Jeannie didn't want to say anything in front of young Christine.

"What about little Jennifer, where's she? Who's looking after her?"

Christine rolled her eyes. She was over the initial shock and could show her impatience.

"Don't worry, Dad. Everything is being taken care of. The Johnsons have got Jennifer over at Wynfords."

When Dan got back to Rickyard Cottage in dry clothes again, he was in time to see Peggy being carried out on a stretcher to a waiting ambulance. The rain was still pouring down and she was covered by a large, black waterproof sheet. Only her face showed. She was conscious now and she gave him a weak smile.

"Sorry I've been such a nuisance, Dad."

"Oh, Peg love, don't even think about it."

He touched her pale cheek gently and then the ambulancemen deftly pushed him aside as they put her in the back of the ambulance.

Doris was standing by watching.

"I think she's going to be all right, Dan. Dr Harvey's sending her to Felpersham just for a bit of a rest and a check-up. He says she'll be on her feet again pretty soon."

"What about the baby?"

She shook her head sadly.

"He's not all that sure about the baby. He thinks it'll be all right but Peg's lost some blood and the shock's not going to do her any good. He says there's no sign of any serious problems, though. He says we won't know for certain for another day or so."

"What about Jack?"

"Jack doesn't know very much about anything at the moment. He's in a dreadful state. He doesn't seem to know what happened to him. He just remembers blacking out. There's an enormous bruise on his chin. Dr Harvey thinks he must have hit the spade handle when he fell over."

Dan went upstairs and quickly told the doctor what had really happened. Dr Harvey smiled at him.

"I don't think we need to go into any detail, Dan. The bruise won't do the lad any harm. It's his chest I'm worried about. It sounds very wheezy, and there's obviously some inflammation there, I just hope it doesn't develop into pneumonia or anything like that. I don't really want to take him into the hospital just yet. I don't suppose there's any chance of Doris looking after him at Brookfield, is there?"

"Of course there is. Doris wouldn't hear of anything else."

When the doctor had gone, Dan and Doris surveyed the mess. The rainwater had now seeped into the cottage and the whole ground floor was covered in about two inches of dirty black water. The smell was awful. Upstairs, a tree branch had been blown against one of the windows and smashed the glass. The rain had already soaked most of the room. The home that Peggy and Jack had so painstakingly created over the past few months had disappeared. Rickyard Cottage was almost as bad as when they'd started.

Dan put his arm round Doris's shoulders.

"What do we do now, lass?"

Doris looked up at him.

"What do the Archers always do? We pick ourselves up, dust ourselves down and start all over again."

"Aye, lass. That's what you and I would do. But what about young Jack and Peg? They've had it very rough for a long time. Do you think they can get over this?"

Doris looked at him again and shook her head.

"I don't think you know our daughter-in-law very well, Dan. She's got much too much spirit to let anything get her down. She'll soon bounce back again, just you wait and see."

CHAPTER EIGHT

The kitchen at Rickyard Cottage looked like a cross between a busy railway station and a department store on Christmas Eve, with a touch of the East End sweatshop thrown in for good measure. In one corner, seated at the treadle sewing machine she'd borrowed from Doris for the occasion, Peggy was hemming a pile of brightly coloured material, while the room was full of her friends from the Women's Instititue bustling to and fro with great armfuls of bunting. Outside in the yard, Jack and his mates from The Bull were hard at work hammering and sawing and banging in nails, in between swigging the odd pint of ale.

Ambridge was preparing to celebrate the Royal Wedding in style, ready this day at least to cast aside ration books, clothing coupons and all the other privations of post-war England. The fairy-tale romance between the young Princess Elizabeth and her handsome Greek prince had captured the country's imagination as nothing else had done since the end of the war, and their wedding had provided the first real excuse for the people to let their hair down.

To Peggy's surprise, Jack had been elected chairman of the the village's organising committee. Organisation and planning weren't exactly his strong points, and she could only presume he'd been chosen because of the way he'd overcome his terrible problems earlier in the year. He'd become something of a local hero. Despite being uninsured against damage and loss, Jack had set about re-building his smallholding, ignoring his health problems and working from morning until night to repair the havoc caused by the terrible snow and floods of the winter.

By the time their second baby, Lilian, was born in July, Jack was back on top of things to such a degree that he'd even been able to hide his bitter disappointment that it was another girl! However, despite Peggy's pride that he'd been chosen to organise the celebrations, to her it was all a terrible mistake since Jack had immediately volunteered their little cottage as the centre of operations. Of all the houses in the village, Rickyard Cottage was probably the least suitable headquarters.

There was hardly room to swing a cat in either the kitchen or the front parlour at the best of times. Now, with the constant stream of people tramping in and out with armfuls of material to be made up into costumes, Peggy was beginning to feel she'd have been better off living in the middle of Piccadilly Circus. There'd have been more room there.

For weeks now, the preparations had disrupted the normal routines of the family. If Peggy hadn't been able to leave Jennifer and Lilian at Brookfield for most of the day, she would probably have gone mad. She loved being at the centre of things, but this was ridiculous. She'd discovered the hard way that farming folk don't work to the same sort of timetable as people in the city. It was nothing unusual for someone to be knocking on the door at seven o'clock in the morning wanting the use of the sewing machine because they happened to have an hour or two to spare between milking and feeding the chickens.

That's how this morning had started, and things had got steadily crazier as the day had gone on. Egged on by Jack, the committee had decided that a huge party wasn't sufficient for Ambridge to mark the event – they had agreed to put on a historical pageant and an evening's entertainment as well. Having heard part of the script that had been written by George Timms, the village school headmaster, Peggy personally thought hysterical would have been a more appropriate word to describe the pageant, but she kept this opinion to herself. Now the great day was approaching with alarming speed and Jack kept remembering things that should have been done weeks before, throwing everyone else into confusion.

The latest panic had arisen because Elsie Catcher discovered that Jack hadn't told any of the costume-makers about the scene describing Ambridge's Roman past which required half a dozen togas and tunics. Luckily a quick hunt through the village had produced enough old sheets to fit the bill. Now the sewing machine and the cutting scissors were being used flat out, saving Jack from another red face.

Above the whirring and clicking of the sewing machine, Peggy heard a sudden yell. All the banging in the yard stopped and Jack appeared in the doorway with a pained expression on his face . . . and blood dripping from a gash on his forehead. Peggy examined the cut anxiously.

"What on earth have you done this time?"

Jack was accident-prone. The day before, he'd cracked his shin on some wooden contraption he'd just created and that morning he'd managed to jam his finger in the latch on the back door.

"The 'ead's come off me 'ammer and caught me a pearler on the bonce. Could you do a running repair on it for me?"

Peggy smiled. If he could joke about it, it wasn't as serious as she'd feared. Jack still liked to slip the occasional bit of Cockney slang into his own conversation to tease Peggy, as if to remind her how quickly she had lost her accent. She rewarded him in kind.

"Cor, luv-a-duck . . . you look like a geezer wot's just run inter a brick wall."

As she patched him up, she could smell the sourness of the beer on his breath. She constantly worried about the amount he seemed to drink, but she knew better than to say anything.

"Why don't you sit down and take it easy for a while, Jack? And I'll make a cup of tea. They reckon hot, sweet tea is the best thing for shock."

Jack grinned wickedly.

"No, ta luv . . . I've got me own cure for shock."

From the inside pocket of his jacket, he brought out a small flask and before she could say anything he'd taken a long swig of whisky.

She decided to ignore it.

"How are things going outside? Are we going to be ready for the big day?"

"Of course we'll be ready. You're not harbouring any doubts about your husband's abilities to keep to a simple timetable are you?"

Although he was still smiling, he sounded slightly touchy, and Peggy suspected he was beginning to get nervous.

"Come on, Jack, I asked a simple question. I wasn't making any insinuations. I was just wondering how it was all going."

"Well, it's going very well. We've finished building the scenery and we'll start painting it this afternoon . . ."

Elsie Catcher, the young schoolteacher, looked up from the sewing machine.

"Did you remember that extra tableau in the pageant we talked about?"

"Er . . . yes, but . . . um . . . we didn't have enough wood for that. Our Phil's promised to get some from the estate."

Peggy wasn't sure why Jack was looking shifty. It could simply have been that he'd forgotten about the extra tableau and was just covering up for himself, but at times she felt quite uneasy about his relationship with Elsie, especially now they were working together so closely on the pageant. Sometimes when she talked to him, the schoolmistress sounded almost like Jack's wife!

"You've forgotten all about it, haven't you? Why don't you admit it, Jack Archer? You've got a memory like a cracked beer glass."

The rest of the women in the kitchen laughed. It was a very appropriate remark. Jack put on a hangdog look.

101

"I'm sorry, Elsie. You're right, of course. It had slipped my mind for the moment, but now that you've reminded me so graciously, I'll have it attended to right away."

He hurried back outside and a minute or two later a great groan went up. He'd obviously broken the bad news to his mates.

Young Susan Grundy giggled.

"Jack doesn't sound none too popular out there! What's this new tableau you were talking about, Elsie? When did the idea come up? My Joe was at the committee meeting last night and he never mentioned nothing about it."

Elsie Catcher blushed. The idea hadn't come up at the committee meeting, but afterwards when Jack had walked her home. She decided the where and when bit should be avoided.

"Oh, Mr Timms and I were talking about the pageant and we suddenly realised there was a chance to tie in Ambridge's history with the history of England by having a tableau representing our local heroes coming back from the Great War."

"That sounds like a good idea."

"Yes, as Mr Timms was saying, there are quite a lot of men in the village who took part in that war and we thought it only right to mark their great contribution to Ambridge and their country."

Peggy smiled. Sometimes the pretty Miss Catcher sounded much more of a schoolmistress than a potential siren.

"What will the tableau show, Elsie?"

The other women were also interested.

"Which of the heroes are you going to have, then?"

"You've got to have George Grundy!"

"Don't forget Percy Hood."

"What about asking Brigadier Winstanley?"

"What are you going to do about uniforms?"

"Aren't they all a bit old to look like heroes now?"

Elsie was taken aback by all the questions. The truth was she hadn't thought it through properly and, despite what she'd said, she hadn't even mentioned it to Mr Timms. He might not like the idea because of all the extra work it would entail. It was too late to worry about that now, however. She'd just have to use her persuasive charms on him.

"I can't answer all your questions because that part of the script isn't written yet. But I don't think we'd want to use the actual men themselves because, as somebody said, they probably wouldn't look right. We thought we'd ask one or two of the younger men instead."

"Who?"

"How about my Joe? He'd look grand in uniform."

There were one or two stifled laughs. His father might have been a sergeant major, but Joe Grundy was probably the scruffiest lad in the village. He was handsome enough, but the thought of him smartening up enough to wear an army uniform with any kind of style was inconceivable. No one, however, wanted to upset Susan and other names were hurriedly thrown into the discussion.

"The Allard lads would look good."

"Yes, and what about the young vet?"

"There's Jethro Larkin. Or is he a bit too young?"

"Don't forget young Paul Johnson!"

Peggy paused before she said anything. She was beginning to wonder if this idea might be one way of giving her Jack the welcome home he'd always felt should have been his. She'd never forgotten their bumpy ride to Ambridge from Hollerton Junction at dead of night seated next to Phil on the old pony trap, and she suspected Jack still felt bitter about the manner of his return.

"My Jack's still got his uniform from the last war. I don't know if it'd fit him now, but if it doesn't I'm sure he'll gladly lend it to someone else. It'll save on the sewing!"

Elsie Catcher was quick to grasp the suggestion.

"That's the answer! Why don't we ask two or three of the men from the last war to take the parts of their fathers or grandfathers?"

There was a chorus of agreement. At least it would save on having to sew any more costumes.

"I wonder if it's as chaotic as this at Buckingham Palace?"

Betty Barrett had just arrived and was surveying the apparent confusion in the tiny kitchen. Peggy tried to sound slightly aggrieved.

"It only *looks* chaotic, Betty. We've actually got everything under control . . . or at least we had, until we discovered there was another little thing our Jack had forgotten to mention to us. I expect it won't be all that much better at Buckingham Palace. I read in the paper the other day that Princess Elizabeth still hadn't decided on what kind of wedding dress she wanted."

Susan Grundy looked dreamy.

"I bet she's ever so excited now. I know I was when I was trying to decide what to wear."

Susan was the most recently married of the girls and everyone remembered how several of her neighbours had made a collection of clothing coupons to help her to get a decent outfit.

"At least she won't have any worries about having enough clothing coupons for her trousseau."

Peggy shook her head.

"You're wrong there, Susan. The paper said she might have to settle for a calf-length dress because she hadn't been able to save up enough coupons for anything more."

Betty Barrett couldn't believe it.

"That's rubbish. It's just typical newspaper gossip. Fancy the Royal Family not being able to do exactly what they please just because we've got a Labour government. King George wouldn't stand for that and I'm positive the Queen wouldn't allow any nonsense from the politicians."

"No, honestly, it's true, Betty. It was the *Daily Herald* I saw it in and you can hardly imagine it being on her side, can you?"

Susan Grundy looked sad.

"I think that's terrible. You can't have a royal wedding with the bride not having a long dress and a great flowing train. Blow all the coupon business. I reckon they ought to make an exception in this case!"

Peggy nodded in agreement.

"I'm sure you're right, Susan, but I can't imagine that they'll allow it, all the same. The Royal Family have got to set an example. It would never do for them to be seen to splash out while the rest of the country is having a hard time. Anyway, Princess Elizabeth will look gorgeous whatever she wears!"

Outside in the yard, the men had weightier matters on their minds.

"How much beer do you think we'll need?"

It was Tom Forrest who asked the question, the committee having made him responsible for the liquid refreshments. Jack looked at the row of empty flagons sitting on the yard wall.

"If you lot are going to drink at anything like the same rate as you've done today, I reckon we'll need all the beer The Bull and The Cat and Fiddle can let us have!"

Sam Crowcroft looked apprehensive.

"Hang on a minute, Jack. You're not suggesting that I donate all the beer, are you? I know I promised to let you have as many barrels as you wanted, but I didn't . . ."

Jack grinned and interrupted him.

"There you are, Uncle Tom. We've got a very generous offer from Sam, here . . . and I'm sure the men of the village will be very grateful to you Sam. I should imagine you'd gain a host of new customers from such generosity. I don't think we'll even have to approach The Cat and Fiddle after all."

Sam had been the landlord of The Bull much too long to be caught out by someone like young Jack Archer.

"I don't need any new customers, thank you very much! You lot are quite thirsty enough to keep me in a comfortable living. It's The Cat and Fiddle that needs to lure in customers. Let Joe Slade provide you with some free beer. Mind you, I'm not sure many folk will want to drink his watered-down rubbish, even if it is free!"

Tom Forrest was enjoying the banter – but he was also due at the church to supervise the bell-ringing practice.

"All right, let's be serious for five minutes. How much beer are we going to need?"

Walter Gabriel intervened.

"If Sam and Joe Slade are going to be tight-fisted about it, I'd be quite happy to supply you with a few gallons of me own brew as my donation towards the celebrations."

It sounded like an offer he couldn't refuse, but having sampled too many glasses of Walter's home-brewed special, Tom Forrest knew he would have to resist, if the men of Ambridge were to remain sober for more than half an hour on the wedding day.

"That's very decent of you, Walter, but it wouldn't be fair to let you do that. You're making a big enough contribution as it is."

It was an acceptable get out because Walter had already helped with the stage scenery and his wife, Annie, had sacrificed several pairs of curtains to help make costumes.

"But, Tom, I'd be real happy if my ale was to be drunk by all my friends and neighbours on such a special occasion."

Tom gave way.

"Righto, Walter. I'm not the man to turn down an act of generosity. How much do you think you'll be able to provide?"

He needed to know how much of the lethal brew he'd somehow have to get rid of without offending Walter.

106

"I've got about forty gallons already, but I could make some more before the day . . ."

"No, no, Walter, don't you make any more! I was only joking when I said I wouldn't be donating any beer from The Bull. Of course I will."

Sam Crowcroft saw the danger to his regular customers. They were liable to go blind after three or four pints of the Gabriel concoction. He reckoned it was drinking too much of it that had made Walter one of the village eccentrics!

With another crisis averted, Tom felt free to go off to his bell-ringing, but Jack stopped him.

"Just before you disappear, Uncle Tom, could we run through the evening's entertainment for the programme?"

"Aye, lad, but it'll have to be quick because I've got folk waiting for me at the church. We've got an awful lot of practising to do if we're to get the wedding peal right."

Tom took his bell-ringing very seriously. He'd been at it since he was a lad of ten and in the last couple of years since the end of the war, he'd spent half his spare time trying to establish a proper Ambridge team. He never quite made it. Whenever he got close to having a full group, somebody would either lose interest or go off and get married or move away or something. The result was that almost every able-bodied person in the village had been bored rigid at one time or another by Tom's lectures on the fascinating subject of change-ringing and all the many mathematical permutations possible during a single peal.

Jack dreaded to think what complications the wedding peal would cause Tom's band of volunteers over the next few days, but he already had more than enough to worry about.

"All I needed to know was what you were planning to do as your party piece. The squire's agreed to act as MC and I'm seeing him tonight to give him some idea of what's happening and what he needs to do about introducing folk."

Tom looked surprised.

"You're not expecting me to do owt other than 'The Village Pump' are you?"

Tom Forrest had been singing the same song at village events almost as long as he'd been bell-ringing. It had become something of a joke . . . but not one Jack appreciated. He'd been hoping for something different for the royal wedding concert.

"Well, if you're going to do that again, Uncle Tom, is there any chance of changing one or two of the verses?"

"What do you mean?"

"It's not exactly a wedding kind of song, is it? I wondered if maybe you could rewrite it a little bit to make it more appropriate for the occasion?"

"I haven't got time to mess around with the words now, lad. I've got the bells to sort out. If you think 'The Village Pump' isn't good enough for your concert, then it's all right by me if you drop it from the programme."

Jack might have been tempted to agree, but Walter Gabriel certainly wouldn't hear of that.

"Don't be daft, Tom. The concert wouldn't be a concert if you weren't there singing 'The Village Pump'. You'm be the star of the show, usually. Don't you'm listen to the boy, me old pal, me old beauty. You sing as you allus does."

Sometimes Jack wondered if he really was in charge or not. Nobody seemed to take a blind bit of notice of anything he said, but he was always getting it in the neck when things went wrong. Maybe that's all being in charge meant . . . being the scapegoat!

"While you're deciding what's going to be in the concert that I'm supposed to be in charge of, perhaps you could let me in on your intentions, Walter?"

"No need to get all huffy and sensitive with me, lad. There are certain traditions in the village that you ought not to mess around with, and your Uncle Tom is one of them. You ask your mother if you don't believe me."

Jack groaned. Asking simple questions in a place like Ambridge was a hazardous undertaking. You never knew quite what you were letting yourself in for.

"Thank you for the advice, Walter. I'll gladly take it . . . but I would still like to have some idea of what you're going to be doing on the night. Please?"

"Ned Larkin and I have got a duet lined up."

"A duet? Both of you singing, you mean?"

Jack couldn't believe it. Walter Gabriel had a speaking voice like a corncrake and Ned Larkin always sounded as if his false teeth didn't fit him. The thought of them trying to sing was amazing enough. The thought of them trying to sing in unison, let alone in harmony, was positively out of this world. Was Ambridge ready for this, he wondered.

"How exactly would you like the squire to introduce you then? I mean, do you want him to warn the audience . . . I mean inform the audience that you're going to sing a duet? Or would you rather leave it as a surprise?"

Walter was not amused. He replied with affronted dignity.

"Me and my pal Ned have gone to a lot of trouble to learn the words of our song and we'll want a proper introduction from the squire. But we don't want to be immodest and push ourselves forward. We're going to dream up a couple of stage names and we'll let you have them afore the day, don't you worry."

"What about accompaniment?"

"What d'you mean, accompanimament?"

Walter always somehow managed to add an extra syllable to long words.

"Me and Ned will be accompanying each other, I just told you that!"

Jack gave up yet another unequal struggle. He was unlikely to get any sense out of Walter . . . or Ned, come to that. He could only hope that it would be all right on the night.

At least he could be sure that his mum and dad wouldn't let him down. He'd heard them practising their parts often enough to know that they'd be in fine voice for the concert. He wasn't completely sure that young Phil would be up to playing the piano for them, though Jack had only ever heard him playing the organ at church and he'd been about as good as the St Stephen's choir, which wasn't saying much.

Peggy came out into the yard to say that most of the women had finished their work for the day and were going home. Walter and the other men took the hint and they, too, drifted away. Jack put his arm round his wife's waist.

"Well, how are you enjoying being in the thick of village life, Peg? Does it all seem very petty to you?"

"You know me better than that, Jack. I love Ambridge. This is my home now. All these people are our friends and what friends do together is never petty."

"Maybe not, but if you were back in London now you would be planning to go to some fancy celebration at the Hammersmith Palais or somewhere posh. You wouldn't be thinking of marking the royal wedding with an amateur concert that would die a horrible death in the Naafi at Aldershot and with a pageant written in a school exercise book by the local headmaster."

Peggy stretched up and kissed him.

"If I was in London, I would be just part of a great anonymous mass waiting for other people to show me how to enjoy myself. I'd follow the crowd. Here in Ambridge, I'm Peggy Archer . . . whose husband is so well liked and respected that we've been given the privilege of helping everyone else in the village to enjoy a very special day. So just you stop all this silly talk, Jack Archer."

CHAPTER NINE

Peggy was washing up and feeling pretty fed up when she heard Jim Price come whistling down the lane. Ambridge's postman was one of nature's cheerful souls. She was depressed because the rain was coming down in buckets, but minor irritations like that never seemed to bother him. He whistled and sang on his daily round whatever the weather. She heard the letterbox rattle and dried her hands on her overall as she went out into the hall to collect whatever letters he'd dropped on the mat.

There was nothing there.

Surprised, she opened the door to find Jim standing outside looking a little bit like a drowned rat, but with a broad grin on his face. He was holding a single letter and he waved it at her.

"I reckon this one might be worth a cup of tea, Peggy. It's all the way from New Zealand . . . nice colourful stamp on it. My Ethel says it's a new one she hasn't seen before."

Ethel, Jim's wife, was the village postmistress, and stamp-collecting was her favourite pastime. Peggy got the hint.

"If you don't mind waiting until I've had a look at it myself, you can have it for Ethel!"

Jim looked guilty. He'd got so used to cadging stamps that he wasn't really aware of doing it any more.

"I'm sorry, Peggy, I didn't mean to be rude. It's just that most people don't even notice what stamps are on the envelopes and it seems such a waste when Ethel gets so much pleasure from them."

The Prices had moved into Ambridge about a year earlier. Countrypeople from Gloucestershire, they had fitted in very well.

"Don't worry, Jim. I was only teasing. Come in and have a cup of tea."

"Are you sure you've got the time, Peggy, because I was only joking about that, too?"

"For goodness sake come in and stop rabbiting on, Jim. I'll just put the kettle on. I need a cup of tea to cheer me up. Doesn't this rain get you down?"

Jim dumped his heavy mailbag on the floor and sat down at the big pine kitchen table.

"To tell you the truth, Peggy, I can't afford to take any notice of the weather. If I bothered about a spot of rain, it would take me twice as long to do my round. Then again, if I let myself enjoy the sunshine too much I wouldn't want to hurry and so that would take me twice as long as well!"

It was a philosophy Peggy only half agreed with. She'd be happy to ignore the rain, but she certainly wouldn't want to miss out on the pleasure of feeling the summer sun on her face! Maybe postmen weren't really as cheerful as they sounded.

"The cottage seems very quiet this morning, Peggy. What have you done with the kids?"

"Well, you won't believe it but they're upstairs fast asleep. They were both awake at the crack of dawn this morning. Jennifer came bouncing into our bed just as the dawn chorus was getting under way and she's been on the go ever since. I only put her down to sleep about ten minutes ago so I'm keeping my fingers crossed she'll sleep for at least an hour or so."

"And how old is the baby? Must be nearly a year now?"

Peggy grinned.

"Not bad for a man, Jim Price. It's Lilian's birthday tomorrow!"

The postman looked shamefaced as he held out four large envelopes addressed to Lilian.

"I have to confess these gave me a bit of a clue! I knew her birthday was around about now, but there weren't quite enough cards here for it to be today. You get to know these things, you see. I'd guess that one of these early cards is from your mother. She'd have posted it in plenty of time so that she wouldn't miss the actual day. The others are probably from equally nervous relatives who don't trust the GPO!"

Peggy looked at the envelopes. One was postmarked London and was in her mother's awful scrawl. Two were from Bournemouth where both her father's sisters had gone to live, and the fourth was from Cornwall. She recognised the writing but couldn't quite place it.

"Well, you've got at least three out of four correct. I'm not sure about the fourth. I'll let you know tomorrow! What about the New Zealand one? Have you worked out who that's from?"

Jim pulled a face.

"That one's no challenge at all. It's from your Aunt Laura. She's put her name and address on the back."

Peggy laughed and poured the tea. There was no use trying to keep anything secret in a small place like Ambridge.

After Jim left, Peggy picked up the letter from New Zealand. She was surprised to see it was addressed to her. Why hadn't Aunt Laura written to Jack? She'd never written to her – Jack always signed the card they sent at Christmas from them both. As she opened it, she was even more surprised to see a postal draft fall out. It must be another early gift for little Lilian. That was nice of her.

She looked at the draft again. It was for £1,000.

There must be some mistake. She knew Jack's aunt and uncle in New Zealand were well off, but surely they wouldn't have sent £1,000 as a birthday present for a one-year-old!

When she read the letter, she discovered there was no mistake, though. Aunt Laura really had meant to enclose the money . . . but it wasn't for the baby. It was for her and Jack, to help them get over all the problems caused by the previous winter's weather. She looked at the letter again and re-read it slowly.

Dear Peggy,
    I hope you won't mind me writing to you personally. I know it's not quite polite since we've never met but I hope you will forgive me because

it's only the long distance between us that's stopped that. I feel that I do know you because my sister-in-law, Doris, has told me all about you in her letters.

Frank and I were very distressed to hear about all the trouble you have had in trying to get your smallholding under way. It must have been especially awful for you when the weather wrecked all your valiant efforts. I must admit I cried when I read Doris's letter telling us about it all.

I don't know how much you've heard about Frank and me . . . probably not a lot if it's been left to nephew Jack. If he's anything like the rest of the Archer men, he won't have said much. Anyway, the point is that Frank and I have never really had any problems. We took over my dad's sheep-farm a few years after we got married and we've had it pretty comfortable ever since. That makes me feel very guilty when I hear the struggle you and Jack have had. We've never been lucky enough to have children of our own, so I hope you won't take it amiss if we offer you the help that we would give our own family.

Frank tells me young Jack won't accept the money I've enclosed and that's why this letter is addressed to you. It's up to you to make him see sense. We can afford the gift and we both want you to have it. Don't accept any mealy-mouthed protests from my nephew. Or you tell him that I'll personally come over to Ambridge to sort him out!

Actually I really would like to come to England and visit you all. Frank talks almost endlessly about the English countryside and how beautiful it is but whenever I suggest we come over he claims to be too busy. One of these days it'll be different, and you'll find a couple of Kiwis on your doorstep.

In the meantime, you make Jack keep the money. I know you'll make good use of it. It would be nice to hear from you if you ever have the time to sit down and write.

Your New Zealand aunt

Laura

PS I would send my love to your kids, but they wouldn't know who the blazes I was! Uncle Frank sends his love, too.

Peggy felt the tears stinging her eyes as she read the letter for the third time. She'd heard very little about this Aunt Laura. She knew a bit more about Uncle Frank. He was Dan's youngest brother and he'd gone to New Zealand instead of joining up during the First War. Out there, he'd got a job on a sheep-farm and eventually married the farmer's daughter. No one had ever talked about him being wealthy, but then nobody had ever spoken about him much, and Peggy had never given any thought to him, to be honest. No more than she had to Dan's other brother, Ben, who was living somewhere in Canada.

Aunt Laura was right about Jack, though. He wouldn't be happy about accepting the money, and she'd be partly to blame for that. When they'd first moved to Brookfield, Peggy had gone on and on about not scrounging off his parents so that Jack was now reluctant to go there even for Sunday lunch. Not that there'd been many invitations to Brookfield recently.

For some reason, Peggy wasn't quite sure why, things had got quite strained between Jack and his father. It seemed to have something to do with the flood and the time she'd been taken so bad. Since then Dan almost seemed embarrassed to look Jack straight in the eye. Doris, of course, had rushed round to lend a hand when Lilian was born, offering to take Jennifer off her hands, but father and son had certainly drifted apart. In fact, Peggy couldn't think when Jack had last been to Brookfield, and she quite missed Dan's dropping in on her in Rickyard Cottage of a morning for a cup of tea and a bit of a chat.

Peggy looked again at the £1,000 draft. She still couldn't believe it was real. She'd never had so much money in her hand. It must represent something like three years', maybe even four years' wages for the average farmworker. It was too much for Peggy to work out in her head. It didn't really matter. It was certainly one heck of a lot of money.

She heard footsteps in the yard. Jack must be back a bit earlier than usual, but as she was about to rush out to meet him and tell him the news, there was a knock on the kitchen door. It's probably Jim Price, she thought, come back to collect the New Zealand stamp. Then she remembered he never came to the back door. He'd once told her that his Ethel always advised him to go to the door with the letterbox in it. That way he could do the job he was paid to do – deliver letters – without intruding on folks' privacy. Calling at the back door, Ethel had said, could be dangerous, because you might find people in all sorts of situations which they – and he – could find embarrassing.

Opening the door, Peggy saw a tall, bedraggled figure standing on the step, an old army kit-bag slung over his shoulder. He was a dark man, quite handsome, and looked vaguely familiar.

"Hello, Peggy!"

Peggy looked puzzled.

"Well I never, you don't remember me. Fancy that . . . me, the light of your life in the dreary quartermaster's stores for nearly a year and you've forgotten me already. I'm devastated!"

"Barney!"

Ignoring his soggy wet coat, she threw her arms round him and gave him an enormous hug.

"Barney Lee! You look so different out of uniform . . . and you've put on a lot of weight . . ."

"I hope you mean I've broadened out!"

"You look so different. No wonder I didn't recognise you. I can't believe it. Come in. Come in!"

As he peeled off his wet coat, Peggy could see he looked very tired. To get to Ambridge at this time of the morning from anywhere, he must have been travelling all night.

"Sit down and I'll make a cup of tea and get you a bite to eat. I don't suppose you've had much breakfast this morning?"

"Not exactly, Peggy, but a slice or two of toast will do very nicely, thank you."

While she busied herself at the sink and the gas stove, she could feel Barney's eyes on her, and she felt slightly uncomfortable.

"You're looking as gorgeous as ever, Peggy, and having two kids hasn't done your figure any harm either."

Peggy remembered his nickname at Aldershot. It was Blarney!

"Jack should be back any time now. He likes to drop in for a cup of tea about this time. What are you doing in this part of the world anyway, Barney?"

He looked surprised.

"Didn't you get my letter?"

"Letter? No . . . at least I don't think so. Not unless Jack got it and forgot to mention it."

Something suddenly clicked in Peggy's mind. The fourth birthday card . . . from Cornwall.

"Was it inside a birthday card you sent to the baby?"

"Yes, that's right."

"Ah, well you see, it only arrived about half an hour ago and I haven't opened it because it's not Lilian's birthday until tomorrow."

There was a clattering in the yard and this time there was no mistaking who it was. She could hear Jack shouting at the dog. As he opened the door, the animal tried to follow him into the kitchen and in trying to keep it out Jack didn't realise Peggy had company.

"Blasted weather. Thank God we've had the drainage sorted out, otherwise this downpour would have us in the same state as in the winter."

After the flood back in March, the squire had sent a team of men down to dig drainage ditches on Jack's fields.

At last he closed the door successfully, leaving the dog on the outside. Turning round, he suddenly noticed the other man sitting at his table. He stopped and stared.

"Good heavens, Barney Lee! What are you doing here?"

Barney, who'd been sitting watching Jack's prolonged arrival with amusement, stood up and grasped him by the hand.

"Well, that's a fine welcome for an old pal. What do you think I'm doing here? I've come to see my old army mucker . . . and, of course, his gorgeous wife and those two lovely kids you've been raving about in your letters."

Jack pumped his hand enthusiastically.

"It's terrific to see you Barney. You look great."

Jack and Barney had found themselves in the same boat at Aldershot. Like Jack, Barney had been declared medically unfit for active service by a young MO. He'd never found out what was supposed to be wrong with him, but it wasn't bad enough to earn him a discharge. Naturally enough, he and Jack had teamed up together as they'd waved goodbye to all the other lads whose chances of military glory hadn't been knocked on the head by the doctors.

Unlike Jack, Barney had stayed on in the army until the end of the war and then he'd gone to work on a farm in Cornwall. They'd kept in touch through the odd letter, but had never kept their promise to meet up again . . . until now.

"So how long are you staying for, Barney?"

"You haven't read my letter."

"Letter? What letter? I haven't heard from you in ages."

Peggy explained about the letter being inside the birthday card which had only arrived that morning and hadn't been opened yet. In the confusion, she forgot all about the other letter from New Zealand.

Jack waved the explanation aside impatiently.

"Well, never mind all that. It doesn't matter now. Tell us what you're here for, Barney."

"The thing is, Jack, I'm looking for a job. Things haven't worked out too well for me in Cornwall. Don't get me wrong . . . it's a great place and I love it. The farm where I worked was smashing, but . . . well you see . . ."

He looked guiltily at Peggy and actually blushed.

"Well . . . er . . . I had been going out with this local girl and we'd got quite a thing going and . . . um . . . it's a bit difficult in front of Peggy. I'm sorry, love . . . but I sort of got the girl into trouble. She just happened to be the daughter of the biggest farmer in the district, and I'm afraid it was a case of scarpering before I got caught up in one of those old-fashioned double-barrelled shotgun affairs."

Jack laughed and slapped him on the back.

"Well, well. The same old Barney. You always were a rogue and they say the leopard never changes its spots."

"Ah, but I have changed spots . . . from Cornwall to Borsetshire. Now tell me, what are the prospects around here . . . for finding a job that is!"

They all laughed.

"I was rather hoping that you might put me up for a bit while I scouted around for something. Do you know of anything going in the area?"

Jack shook his head.

"Not really. I tend to get a bit blinkered working on the smallholding so I'm afraid I've got no idea if anybody's looking for help, but I'll ask around. There's bound to be some work available for a good man like you. As for accommodation . . . that's no problem at all. You can stay here for as long as you like. That's all right, isn't it Peg?"

119

Peggy was flustered. The spare bedroom was a mess. While she'd been redecorating the cottage before Lilian was born it had been used as a kind of glory hole, and it was still piled high with all sorts of rubbish. She hadn't even opened the door in weeks.

Jack was quick to jump on her hesitation.

"There's no problem about that, is there? I mean, we managed very well when your mother came to stay and she was here for the best part of a month."

That was true enough. Her mum had come for a week just after Lilian was born, but she'd enjoyed herself so much she'd stayed longer. Peggy felt guilty because Jack had made her mum feel really at home. He'd gone out of his way to introduce her to people around the village and he'd even bought her a bunch of flowers for all the work she'd done while Peggy was finding her feet again. Of course she'd sort things out now to make Barney's stay as comfortable as possible.

The noises coming from upstairs clearly meant that both children had woken up, and Peggy went to bring them down. Little Jennifer was quickly at ease with "Uncle Barney" and clambered happily onto his lap. Barney looked very much at home as he made all the appropriate remarks about what smashing kids they were.

The rest of Peggy's day disappeared in a frenzy of activity. She made lunch for Jack and Barney while they relaxed and reminisced over a glass of beer, and then fussed around looking after the children. By the time the lunch was over, it had stopped raining and the two men went off for a grand tour of the smallholding.

As soon as she was able, Peggy rushed upstairs to try to sort out the spare bedroom. The mess that greeted her when she opened the door was much worse than she'd feared. There were leftover rolls of wallpaper, half-used tins of paint and paint brushes still soaking in turpentine. The ladders and the board they'd used for pasting the wallpaper were propped against the wardrobe and the bed was piled high with boxes and old clothes. It took her two hours just to sort through the chaos, transferring stuff to the children's room, their own room and every other corner of the house where she could find some space.

Even when she'd finished, she thought the room still looked as if a bomb had hit it. The wallpaper around the window was stained from where the rain had seeped in and the linoleum was heavily marked and cracked. She didn't have a shade for the electric light and the bare bulb looked horribly stark. There were suitcases and boxes stacked on top of the wardrobe and stuffed under the bed.

The "guest" room didn't exactly match up to a bedroom at The Ritz! Mind you, what more could Barney Lee expect, dropping in out of the blue the way he had? Peggy felt resentment creeping over her. It was all very well for Jack to point out that they'd been able to accommodate her mother without any problems, but her mother wasn't a virtual stranger and her presence hadn't meant Peggy having to be careful about getting properly dressed before she could even get to the bathroom.

Back from the guided tour, Jack grinned proudly as Barney said how impressed he was by the smallholding and reeled off a list of its outstanding features, down to the little black and white border collie Jack had trained as a sheepdog.

"Beautifully behaved animal, that Mack."

Little Jennifer was quick to chide him.

"He's not Mack . . . he's Kenzie."

At three and a half, Jennifer was still lisping slightly and Barney couldn't understand what she meant. Peggy had to help.

"The dog's name is Mackenzie. Plain Mack wasn't good enough for our Jack. He'd always wanted a dog of his own and when he finally bought one, he decided he wanted a posh name for it. Mackenzie actually started off his new life at Rickyard Cottage as Mr Mackenzie!"

Barney laughed.

"How did you come up with that, Jack?"

Peggy giggled.

"When he was looking it over at the breeder's, he heard the kennelmaid call it Mr and he thought that was the dog's name. He didn't realise the poor girl was so busy with her animals that she called them all Mr or Mrs or Miss! By then it was too late, the name Mr Mackenzie had stuck."

"But you've dropped the Mr handle now?"

Jack blushed and Peggy giggled again.

"That's another story in itself."

Barney was intrigued but Jack was less anxious to hear the tale.

"You don't want to go through all that nonsense again, Peggy. Barney isn't interested in boring details like that."

"Oh but I am, Jack. It sounds intriguing. Tell me about it, Peggy. Please."

Peggy continued.

"Our local vet is a Scotsman and when Jack took the dog along for its injections, the new receptionist asked its name. Jack said it was Mr Mackenzie, and she told him not to be stupid – it was the dog's name she wanted. He said that *was* the dog's name, and she roared with laughter and told everyone else in the waiting-room about it. Jack's never got over the embarrassment and poor Mackenzie's lost his title!"

Jack remembered the scene in the vet's waiting-room only too well, and he quickly changed the subject.

"Make us another bite to eat, Peg, there's a good girl."

Peggy made a lot more noise than usual as she prepared supper, banging down the pots and pans with much greater force than was needed. She was annoyed that Barney's presence meant that she'd still not been able to talk to Jack about the letter from Aunt Laura. Neither Jack nor Barney noticed her frustration though.

While the men ate, she took the children upstairs to get them ready for bed. As she was tucking Jennifer in, Jack came up to say his goodnights. To her relief, Barney stayed downstairs.

"Oh Jack, I'm so glad to get you on your own at last!"

"Come on, Peg, don't be like that. It's not every day an old pal turns up out of the blue. You can't expect me to leave him on his own."

"No, of course not. That's not what I meant. It's just that we've had this fantastic letter from Aunt Laura and . . ."

Jack glanced at the bedroom clock.

"A letter from Aunt Laura? That's nice, Peg, but tell me about it later."

"But Jack, it's . . ."

"Please, Peg . . . leave it for now. I want to take Barney down to The Bull for a quick drink."

Peggy could see she was wasting her time.

"Yes, sure . . . you've got to look after good old Barney . . . take him for a quick drink. I'll see you tomorrow!"

Jack didn't notice the sarcasm in her voice.

"I was just thinking, Peg . . . what would you say to us offering him a job here?"

Thoughts of the £1,000 flew out of the window.

"We can't give him a job. We haven't got a job to give anyone. We couldn't afford to hire anyone."

Jack shook his head.

"But that's where you're wrong, girl. I reckon if we put him up here, we won't have to pay him a full wage and if we all pull our belts in a bit we can just about do it."

Peggy's face was a picture.

"We can't tighten our belts any more. Do you know when I last bought any new clothes for me or the kids? Do you know when I was last able to go to the pictures, or anywhere else for that matter?"

"That's not very nice talk, Peg. Barney's a very good friend down on his luck. We've got to help him."

There was a wheedling tone in Jack's voice.

"Yes, but . . ."

"I mean, look at the way everyone rallied round us when we were in trouble. We can't just take all the time, you know. We've got to give a little as well."

He'd succeeded in making Peggy feel really guilty by now. Barney's feet were as good as under the table. Before Peggy could say anything about the £1,000 Jack had nipped quickly downstairs. He knew when to quit while he was winning. Shortly afterwards, Peggy heard Jack and Barney go off to the pub. She and the kids were left alone in the house. And she had a feeling it wouldn't be the last time while Barney Lee was staying at Rickyard Cottage.

CHAPTER TEN

Peggy couldn't sleep and lay tossing and turning in her bed. She never could drop off while Jack was still out. The bedside clock's loud tick seemed to reverberate through the house, but she didn't need to look at it to know that it was very nearly midnight . . . she'd already peered at it half a dozen times since it had said 11.30. Wherever Jack was, she thought, it wasn't The Bull. Sam Crowcroft would have turfed him and the other regulars out ages ago.

She could hear Jennifer moving restlessly in the next room. She'd been coughing and wheezing quite a bit and Peggy had been up to look at her two or three times already. She was probably excited about Lilian's birthday the next day, Peggy thought. Fortunately she hadn't woken the baby, and the sound of little Lilian's steady breathing was very comforting.

Peggy was beginning to worry about Jack now. An hour earlier, she'd just been angry . . . with Barney Lee for leading Jack astray and with Jack for letting him. She looked at the clock again. It was a few minutes to midnight. Even Jack Slade would have thrown out the heavy drinkers from The Cat and Fiddle by now. Where could they be? What could have happened to them?

Nearly another long, anxious hour had passed before she heard unsteady footsteps in the yard. The two men stumbled noisily into the house talking in what they no doubt imagined to be whispers.

"Do you want a bite to eat, Barney?"

"That would be smashing. What is there?"

"I don't know. I'll get Peg to come down and get us something."

Peggy could scarcely believe her ears. Jack wasn't the most thoughtful husband at the best of times, but to suggest that she get out of bed in the middle of the night to make supper for a couple of drunks was the absolute limit!

Luckily for Jack, Barney Lee appeared to agree.

"You can't get Peg out at this time, Jack. She'll skin us alive if we wake her now. Let's just have some bread and cheese."

Jack, drunk as he was, obviously saw the wisdom of this suggestion and there was a lot of clattering and banging of cupboard doors as he made heavy weather of finding the bread and cheese.

Now that she was no longer worried about his safety, Peggy lay there fuming with frustration – for one thing, she still hadn't been able to tell Jack about the letter from Aunt Laura. All day she'd been longing to share the news of their windfall with someone, and who else if not Jack?

It was another half-hour before Jack crept clumsily into the bedroom. He started undressing in the dark, imagining that he was doing his best not to disturb her but muttering to himself as he had trouble with his bootlaces.

"You can put the light on!"

Jack jumped and looked at her guiltily.

"You still awake then, Peg?"

"Full marks for observation, Jack!"

"Come on, love. Don't be sarcastic. I have been trying not to disturb you. I'm sorry it's a bit late but Barney and I have been having a little drink and talking over old times."

Peggy was going to say something sharp but she held her tongue as he sat on the edge of the bed, blinking sheepishly in the glare of the light. His trousers were round his ankles but he couldn't get them off because he'd forgotten to take his boots off first. His problem now was that he couldn't get at his laces to undo them.

Peggy couldn't help smiling at his predicament and all her crossness evaporated.

"Did you have a nice evening at The Bull?"

"Yes, thank you, Peg . . . and at The Cat and Fiddle . . . and then at Jim Harris's house, too."

126

Peggy was relieved. The Harrises were a pleasant enough family. She'd always thought well of Jim Harris and his sister, Prue, seemed a nice girl, too. If Jack was going to have a late-night drinking session anywhere, she'd rather it was somewhere like the Harris house.

"Was it just you and Barney there?"

"No, no. Uncle Tom was there for a bit but he went soon after Prue went off to bed, and that left us with George Grundy and Percy Hood."

"That's strange company for you, isn't it?"

Jack usually couldn't be bothered to exchange the time of day with people like George and Percy. He didn't have much time for older folk and often said how boring they were, always talking about the last war and Lloyd George and things like that.

"Aye, you're right . . . under normal circumstances. But you see, when we were at The Cat and Fiddle, one of them brought up the First War and before we knew where we were we were re-fighting both the wars. The old 'uns were saying how terrible it was in their day . . . all the carnage and stuff, much worse than this last war, they said. Well, Barney and I told them some of the horror stories we picked up at Aldershot, and about the awful sights we saw coming back from France and places . . . and then we got on to the Atom Bomb and what it did to those Japanese places. We'd have still been at it if Jim Harris hadn't eventually thrown us out because he had to get up early in the morning."

Jack sounded wide awake now and, surprisingly, he was slurring hardly any of his words. Peggy decided he was sober enough to talk about the £1,000. She picked up Aunt Laura's letter, which was lying on the bedside table, and handed it to him.

"Do you think we could sort out the war some other time, Jack? You ought to read this. It's good news."

He took the letter and saw the New Zealand stamp. He was surprised.

"A letter from Aunt Laura? Surely that'll keep until the morning?"

"No, Jack. Please read it now. I've been dying to talk to you about it all day."

"Give over, lass. It's very late and I've got to get up early, don't forget. I'm only going to get a few hours' shut-eye as it is."

Peggy had no sympathy.

"You should have thought of that when you were trying to drink The Cat and Fiddle dry! You've got to read it now. It's important . . . besides, it might just make it a lot easier to get up in the morning. Please . . . just for me, Jack, read it."

He peered at the letter and had some difficulty focusing on the untidy handwriting.

"Aw, heck, love, I can't read this. What's so important about it? Can't you just tell me?"

Peggy impatiently snatched the envelope back and took out the £1,000 draft.

"This is what's important. We've had a windfall."

Jack couldn't take it in.

"What is it?"

"It's £1,000, that's what it is!"

"£1,000? £1,000? For us? From Aunt Laura? There has to be some mistake."

"There isn't any mistake. Read the letter."

Jack shook his head in disbelief as he struggled through the letter. Even after he'd read several passages two or three times, he still couldn't take it in, and it wasn't the drink that was befuddling him now.

"I've never seen so much money, Peg. Most folk work half a lifetime and don't end up with anything like £1,000!"

Sleep was way beyond him now. He struggled to make sense of it all.

"Do you think maybe Aunt Laura and Uncle Frank have sent it to me as the eldest of the family, and it's meant to be shared with Philip and Christine or something like that?"

Peggy, who'd read the letter at least twenty times during the day, shook her head. It was quite clear that

Aunt Laura, at least, intended the money to go to Jack.

"Aunt Laura doesn't mention either of them in her letter, not that Phil and Christine won't be delighted if you want to share it with them, I'm sure – £300 is bound to come in very handy for both of them."

Shortly after leaving the Farming Institute, young Philip had found himself a good job as farm manager for George Fairbrother. A businessman (and reputed to be one of the wealthiest men in the district), he owned a lot of land around Ambridge. It was a plum job for Philip to have landed straight off, but no one was surprised when he did so. No one was surprised, either, when he started paying court to Mr Fairbrother's pretty daughter, Grace. According to the current gossip, marriage was a distinct possibility now. In such circumstances any cash windfall would be useful.

Young Christine had also done very well at school and was now working for the Milk Marketing Board in some technical capacity that Peggy didn't quite understand – it was something to do with testing the quality of the milk before it was collected from the farms. Everybody said it was very important, anyway. However, her main interest in life remained horses. She was always off riding or working at the local stables and every penny she earned seemed to go on buying some new piece of riding gear. She'd be in clover with her third of the money.

Split three ways like that, the £1,000 suddenly didn't seem to go far. Even if their share didn't offer the end to all Peggy's worries about money, it was still very much better than a kick in the pants, and Peggy was delighted that Jack had stopped to think about his brother and sister for once.

"Whatever else we do, we must put it into the bank first thing tomorrow until you decide exactly what you're going to do with it."

Jack grinned and waved the draft at her.

"I've got quite a few ideas already, Peg!"

"So you've definitely decided to accept it?"

"Accept it? Whatever do you mean? Of course I'm going to accept it. You don't want me to send it back, do you?"

"No, of course not, but I thought you might be unhappy about taking money like that. I thought you might refuse it."

"I couldn't do that. I couldn't throw it back in Aunt Laura's face. She'd be very upset."

"I didn't mean that. It's just that I thought . . . well, you're always talking about wanting to be totally independent of your family and standing on our own feet."

She could have said a lot more about Jack's attitude towards his family and his constant moans about the way everyone kept comparing him to his father. She decided now was not the moment. He was in no mood to listen anyway.

"That's the whole point, Peggy my girl. This £1,000 will help us to do exactly that. With that sort of capital we really will be independent."

Peggy sounded hesitant.

"It won't go all that far when you've split it three ways."

"No . . . you're right. Well, we'll have to see about Phil and Christine. Neither of them have got the responsibilities I have, and they've both got good jobs . . . they don't really need the money when all is said and done. Just think – the money will solve all our problems about finding a job for Barney for a while!"

That was not good news as far as Peggy was concerned. She knew there wasn't enough work for two people around the smallholding. Barney Lee's presence would simply give Jack the opportunity of slipping back to his old lazy ways when they were first married and living at Brookfield. But this was not the time for a heart-to-heart on that subject.

"What else have you got in mind?"

"Well we could buy ourselves a little car. That'll come in very handy and it will give you more freedom to get out and about with the kids."

Jack was not in a practical mood. It would be pointless for Peggy to point out that she couldn't drive a car to save her life. She'd had a go once at Aldershot and the experience had frightened her half to death. Now he embarked on some scheme to do with the spare bedroom.

"The spare room is hardly a priority, Jack. We never use it except for storing most of our junk."

"Yes, but all that's changed now that Barney's come to stay, hasn't it? We can't expect him to live in a pigsty now, can we?"

"What do you mean? I thought we were only going to be putting him up for a few days until he found somewhere proper to live."

"Well, I think he's going to be staying a bit longer than that, Peg. There's no point in him working for us and looking for lodgings somewhere else. It'll be ever so much more convenient if he stays here. He's got lots of great ideas, you know, and I think he can be a big help in getting us firmly on our feet."

Peggy's look of despair passed unnoticed.

"He was saying earlier on this evening . . ."

"Before or after you'd been drinking?"

". . . he was saying that one of the great new things some of the farmers down in Cornwall are doing is growing thousands of chrysanthemums and then potting them and selling them at fat profits to the market garden trade. I think it's a terrific idea – and it's something you could easily help with too, Peg. With Aunt Laura's capital to back us, we could start on it right away."

Alarm bells began to ring very loudly in Peggy's head. She knew little about farming, but she did know that one of the things the farmers around Borsetshire didn't grow was flowers! There must be a good reason for that . . . the soil, or the climate or something.

"Selling chrysanthemums in pots? That doesn't sound an agricultural sort of activity to me, Jack. Don't you think you should talk it over with Dad before you go too far?"

All Jack's earlier mellowness had disappeared and this comment of Peggy's could only serve to irritate him.

"There you go again, Peggy. It's always 'talk to Dad about this' or 'talk to Dad about that'. I don't want to talk to him about anything. He's the last person to talk about new ideas with. He's a real stick-in-the-mud over things like that." Peggy knew she was in for an earful now.

"That's one thing I've come to agree with young Phil over. Dad's living in the past. Look at him and his damn horses, for a start. I remember Phil saying a couple of years back that he ought to get rid of them and mechanise completely, but Dad wouldn't listen. Now look where it's left him. Joe Dunnington's even shut down the village smithy to turn it into a garage. Who knows, if he starts selling cars as well as mending them, we might be one of his first customers!"

Cheered up by this last thought, Jack started musing again quite happily and by the time he eventually fell asleep, he'd finally dismissed all idea of sharing the money with his younger brother and sister. By Peggy's reckoning he'd run through enough schemes to spend the whole £1,000 twice over. His carefree attitude worried her – she had visions of the money running through his fingers like water. She couldn't sleep.

She suddenly sat bolt upright. Someone was moving around outside the bedroom. She was just about to rouse Jack when she suddenly remembered Barney Lee. He was obviously trying to find his way to the bathroom. The noise he made disturbed both children, the baby started to whimper and that started Jennifer coughing again.

A few minutes later, Peggy was aware of the tiny figure of Jennifer standing at the bedside.

"I feel sick. Can I have a drink of water?"

Exhausted and half-asleep, Peggy crawled out of bed. As she picked Jennifer up, she was gripped by panic. Her daughter's nightie was wet through with sweat and her little body was burning. There was no doubt that she was running a temperature. It looked like something much more serious than the pre-birthday nerves that Peggy had assumed were keeping the little girl awake earlier in the night.

Hurriedly she carried her out to the bathroom. She couldn't get in. The door was locked . . . and from the awful groaning sounds coming from inside, it was clear that Barney was suffering from all the drink he'd taken in earlier. She banged on the door urgently, but the only response was another loud moan. Angrily, she hurried downstairs to the kitchen and stripped off Jennifer's nightie. She had to resort to sponging down the little girl by standing her in the kitchen sink. She would have words about this with both Barney and Jack in the morning!

By the time she had cooled Jennifer down, there wasn't much of the night left and she took the little girl into her own bed, where Jack was snoring loudly, unaware of the crisis.

Only minutes later, it seemed, the alarm clock went off. She heard Jack grumble and then tumble wearily out of bed. He staggered off to the bathroom, but returned almost immediately.

"I can't get into the bathroom, Peg. The door's jammed."

"It's not jammed. It's locked."

"Locked? How did that happen?"

"It's your friend Barney. He's been in there all night."

"Heck, Peg. Is he all right?"

"To be perfectly honest, Jack, I couldn't care less. Whatever's wrong, he's only got himself to blame. It's only because he had such a skinful last night. If you want to get into the bathroom you'll have to bang the door and wake him up."

Jack grinned and shook his head.

"No, I won't do that. Better to let him sleep it off. I'll go and sort myself out downstairs in the kitchen."

Peggy was slowly losing her patience. Jack's only thought was for his old army pal. He didn't care that Barney's hogging of the bathroom would cause upset for her and the children.

"And what about the rest of us? Did you know that Jennifer was ill in the night and I had to take the poor little soul down to the kitchen and sponge her down in the sink?"

Jack was immediately all concern.

"How is she now? Is she okay?"

He looked down at the sleeping girl and touched her brow.

"My God, Peg, she's got a raging temperature. Why haven't you called Dr Harvey? You better get him in straight away."

"Don't start getting concerned now, Jack Archer. I've been up with her most of the night while you were snoring your beer away. I'll get the doctor to see her just as soon as it's possible. In any case, maybe you could tell me how I could have got the doctor in the night? The nearest kiosk is down in the village and I couldn't leave the kids alone with you in your state."

"That's an idea! Maybe we should use some of the money to get a phone put in the house?"

"We'll have to see about that. But whatever else happens, they're not going to do it this morning so perhaps you'll be good enough to pop in and ask Irene Jenkins to send the doctor round whenever he's free. The surgery opens at eight o'clock."

"Will she be all right until then?"

"She'll be fine, don't worry. It's a pity you weren't awake to worry when Barney wouldn't let us into our own bathroom to look after our sick daughter."

"There's no point taking it out on him. It wasn't his fault she was sick."

Peggy was totally exasperated.

"Don't you start making excuses for him . . . nor for yourself, for that matter. You both stayed out half the night and then came home stinking drunk, expecting me to cook for you . . ."

"No we didn't. We had bread and cheese."

"I heard you, Jack Archer. You said you'd get me up out of bed to cook something for you . . . just as if I was some servant girl."

Jack sensed he had gone too far again, but he was an expert at back-pedalling.

"I'm sorry about Barney, but it was his first night here and the first decent night out he's had in months . . ."

"Don't make excuses for him!"

"No . . . no . . . you're right. It's not fair to you and the kids. I'll have a word with him this evening. I'll make sure it doesn't happen again. I promise you Peg."

If Peggy had had a pound note for every one of Jack's promises, she'd have been able to send Aunt Laura £1,000, not the other way round. She consoled herself by believing that he really did mean it at the time.

"That's all very well, but what are you going to do about him now? You can't leave him in the bathroom if the doctor's going to come round to see Jennifer."

"Righto, girl. I'll get him back into bed and a bit later on you can take him in a bit of breakfast and I'm sure he'll be as right as rain."

Peggy looked at him in amazement.

"Are you serious? You're suggesting that I get him breakfast in bed?"

"Well, it would be nice, seeing as how it's his first real day with us. I'm sure he'd appreciate it."

"Let's get one thing straight, Jack. I am not getting Barney Lee breakfast in bed today or any other day. If he wants to eat, he'll eat where the rest of us eat . . . and when, too. I'll make breakfast in half an hour or so and anyone who's not at the table doesn't eat as far as I'm concerned."

If Jack was thinking of arguing, he changed his mind when Jennifer woke and started coughing. She looked deathly pale and her dark curls clung wetly to her forehead. He watched as Peggy picked her up and gave her a cuddle.

"Shall I go and see if I can rouse the doctor now, Peg? The poor mite looks awful."

"I don't think she's as bad as she looks. She's just got a bit of a fever. She'll be all right once the doctor gives us something to get her temperature down."

After breakfast – for which Barney didn't appear – Jack went off to the doctor's surgery. He was gone a long time and Peggy had done all the washing up and cleaned the kitchen before he got back.

"Did Irene Jenkins give you any idea what time Dr Harvey would be able to call?"

She suddenly noticed that Jack was looking very flustered.

"What's the matter?"

"I haven't been able to see her. There's a big queue outside the doctor's place and I couldn't get near her."

Peggy looked at him in disbelief. Sometimes his impatience could be infuriating. Two or three people in front of him would constitute a big queue to Jack.

"Honestly, Jack, you really are the limit. It's your own daughter that's sick and you couldn't wait a few minutes to get the doctor to call . . ."

"But it wouldn't have been just a few minutes, Peg. I tell you there's a really big queue . . ."

"How many?"

"I don't know – about thirty, I would guess."

"Thirty? Don't be so daft. Dr Harvey wouldn't have thirty people in the surgery in a week let alone in one morning."

Peggy didn't believe him . . . until she went to the surgery herself about quarter of an hour later. Even if there weren't thirty people in the queue, there were a lot more there than she'd ever seen before. Most of them were known to her, and she managed to push her way through them easily enough when she explained that she just wanted to leave a message.

Once inside, she found Irene Jenkins, normally the essence of calmness, looking hot and bothered. She'd lost much of her natural charm as well.

"Yes? What is it? Oh . . . it's you, Peggy. I'm sorry for being so short-tempered but these people are starting to get on my nerves."

"Whatever is the matter, Irene? Is there an epidemic or something?"

"Oh, there's an epidemic all right but it's not something Dr Harvey can cure. It's this new National Health Service. Now that it's free, everybody wants to see the doctor. It looks as if they've been saving up all their aches and pains for months. There's an epidemic of let's-get-something-for-nothing!"

Peggy had forgotten that the new National Health Service had finally got under way just a couple of days earlier, on 5 July 1948. She was excited as anyone that there was going to be free medical treatment from doctors, dentists and opticians, and saw it as a great triumph for Nye Bevan. Even Jack had agreed that it was a great achievement for the Labour Party. It was just that with Aunt Laura's letter, and Barney arriving, she'd clean forgotten that the historic date had arrived.

According to Irene Jenkins, the queue outside Dr Harvey's was typical of what was happening all over the country.

"Honestly, Peggy, you would hardly credit it but some doctors had people queuing outside their surgeries from the early hours on the day it started and it's been like that ever since . . . and the same with dentists. Now that it's free everybody in the country's got bad teeth needing urgent attention!"

Peggy didn't know what to say. She didn't want Irene Jenkins to think she'd only come for the doctor because she wouldn't have to pay.

"Well, you make me feel guilty now, Irene, but honestly I'd forgotten all about it. I only came to ask if the doctor could come to see our Jennifer. She's been running a temperature all night and I'm a bit worried because she's still very feverish this morning."

Irene Jenkins looked at her appointments book and shook her head helplessly.

"I don't know when it'll be, Peggy. As you can see, it's going to take the rest of the morning to deal with this crowd and then the doctor's got a full list of house calls."

"What if we ask him to come privately, Irene? We're more than happy to pay."

"That doesn't come into it any more, I'm afraid. Dr Harvey's decided to join the National Health Service full time. He won't be having any paying patients, I'm afraid."

Dr Harvey hadn't been one of those doctors who'd given only a half-hearted welcome to the new service. When the doctors' professional body had originally voted on the issue, more than half had been against it and even Nye Bevan's persuasive Welsh tongue couldn't win them all round. In the end, many had agreed to take part only if they could still keep some private patients, but Dr Eric Harvey of Ambridge clearly wasn't one of those.

"What can I do, Irene? The child's sick. She needs the doctor!"

Irene Jenkins could detect the rising panic in Peggy's voice.

"Look, I can't promise anything, but I'll do my best to get the doctor to call some time this afternoon. If he can't, I'll ask him for something that'll get her temperature down and I'll bring it round myself."

When Peggy got back home, she found Barney Lee sitting at the kitchen table with Jennifer wrapped in a blanket on his knee. He was trying to persuade her to drink some milk.

"Where's Jack?"

"He's gone off to work, Peggy, but don't get angry please. I told him I'd look after the kids until you got back. I've warmed some milk for Jenny . . ."

138

"Jennifer!"

"Er . . . for Jennifer, but she doesn't seem to want it. She's very hot. Is the doctor coming soon?"

Peggy looked anxiously at the little girl. She was listless and her face seemed flushed and puffy.

"I don't know when he'll be here. They couldn't tell me."

She was too concerned about Jennifer to bother explaining about the queue, the long list of calls and all the problems caused by the new free health service. The baby's birthday presents lay unopened as she took Jennifer back upstairs and put her to bed. They'd have to celebrate some other time. Lilian was too young to know the difference anyway.

It was nearly five o'clock before Dr Harvey finally arrived. He quickly examined Jennifer and took her temperature.

"It's very high, Mrs Archer. How long has it been like that?"

"Ever since last night."

"Has she complained about pains or has she been sick?"

"She hasn't said anything about being in pain, but she was sick in the night and again this morning."

The doctor put his stethoscope to the little girl's chest again.

"She sounds a bit wheezy. I would like to take her to the cottage hospital for a quick check, but I don't think that's going to be possible. They're rushed off their feet with all the people they're having to deal with at the moment . . ."

Peggy interrupted him.

"But I thought this new health service was going to make things better. What's the point of having a free service if you can't get a sick child into hospital?"

Dr Harvey's bedside manner clicked into place.

"Don't worry Mrs Archer, I'm pretty sure it's only a minor inflammation of the lung and we'll soon have it cleared up with a dose of penicillin. You'll look after her better than any of the nurses under the present circumstances. She just needs to be kept in bed for a few days. Get her to drink as much liquid as you can, and I'll call in regularly. If she doesn't start getting better pretty soon, I'm sure we'll get her into the hospital one way or another."

By the time Jack got in for his tea, Jennifer was sleeping a little less fitfully, although she was still very feverish. Once he was sure that the immediate crisis was over, he began again on his plans for spending the money from Aunt Laura. He'd obviously been thinking of nothing else all day.

"I think we need to put most of it into the smallholding, but I don't see why we shouldn't spend a bit of cash on ourselves, Peg. I know it hasn't been easy for you these last few years, and you deserve a treat of some sort. Maybe we could buy a car and then we could all go off for a bit of a holiday."

Peggy liked the thought of getting away from Rickyard Cottage for a while, but she was much more practical than Jack.

"How can we get away? Who'd look after the livestock?"

"Why, Barney of course!"

She'd forgotten about him. Sensing her disapproval, he'd quietly gone off for a long walk during the day and he'd slipped out again immediately after tea so that she and Jack could be alone for a while. Appreciative though she was of his thoughtfulness, she still wasn't any nearer to wanting him on the smallholding.

"Having a break is a lovely idea, Jack, but I really don't think we can just up and leave things to Barney. We have no idea what sort of worker he is, or how good he is as a farmer. I think you really ought to talk it over with Dad before you go any further."

Jack looked grim.

"Let's get it straight, girl. I run this smallholding. It might not be much compared to Brookfield and most of the other farms around here, but it's mine. I started it from nothing. I didn't inherit it like all the others. I want to run it my way. I don't need to talk to my dad about anything . . . especially not now. You're just going to have to get used to the idea that we're independent now, Peg!"

CHAPTER ELEVEN

The bar of The Bull was very quiet and Jack was sitting on his own, staring morosely into his beer. It was the first time in more than six months that he'd been in the pub without his pal, Barney. It wouldn't be the last, however. Barney had just upped sticks and gone back to Cornwall with virtually no warning at all.

Jack heard a clamour behind him as Walter Gabriel came in. Walter never arrived anywhere quietly. He greeted everyone as if they were long-lost friends, loud "old pals" and "old beauties" ringing out around him. Small as the number of regulars was this evening, he still managed to make the place sound crowded.

Ignoring all the empty stools, Walter chose the one next to Jack.

"Mind if I settle my weary old bones next to you, Jack Archer?"

Jack grunted the barest of acknowledgements. He hadn't much to say to Walter. He'd gone to school with Jack's dad so he couldn't be much more than fifty, but with his cackling voice and store of old wives' tales, he always gave Jack the impression of being an old crone. He certainly regarded himself as one of the village elders and needed to be avoided by anyone not in need of advice! Because of his long friendship with Dan, though, he tended to behave as self-appointed honorary uncle to Jack, Philip and Christine.

"No Barney with you tonight?"

This statement of the obvious irritated Jack.

"If he was, there wouldn't be an empty stool, would there?"

Walter cackled as only he could.

"By heck . . . young Jack, you're as cheerful as ever, I see."

Jack grunted again. He really wasn't in the mood for a dose of homespun philosophy. Walter, though, had clearly been sitting at his spinning wheel most of the day and was in a garrulous mood.

"You'm ought to appreciate having a bit of time for quiet reflection on your own. Barney's been like a shadow to you these past few months."

Chance would be a fine thing, thought Jack.

"Where's he gone tonight then? Off with one of his wenches?"

In the months he'd been in Ambridge, Barney had earned a reputation as a bit of a ladies' man and must have been out with every eligible girl within miles. Some folk said he'd even been out with a few who were not so eligible, and if one or two husbands were to find out they'd have been none too happy about it!

"I don't know where he is tonight. He isn't in Ambridge any more."

"You mean he's gone for good? He doesn't work at Rickyard no more?"

Jack realised any prospect of a quiet drink had gone. People would find out sooner or later that Barney had left, so he might as well tell Walter Gabriel. That would at least ensure the whole village knew in next to no time.

"Yes, that's right. He's gone back to Cornwall to work. He got the offer of a very good job and he'd have been daft not to take it."

The truth was that the spot of bother Barney had landed himself in had turned out to be a false alarm. The Cornish farmer's daughter hadn't been pregnant after all. It had taken Barney a long time to find out because, of course, he hadn't told anyone where he was living. Once he had discovered he was in the clear, he'd written to his old boss who'd been very happy to offer him his job back. Jack had only found out two days earlier that Barney was planning to leave Ambridge. He'd gone that morning while Jack was out working and Peggy and the kids were down in the village, without saying goodbye to any of them. Typical of Barney, that.

"Well, if you'm want my opinion, Jack lad, you're well shot of him. That place of yours ain't big enough to support your family and him. I knows, 'cos I've often thought about getting someone in to help me, but it just ain't economical. An extra hand runs away with all the money."

Jack knew Walter was right, but he wasn't going to admit it. He'd enjoyed having Barney around. He'd worked very hard and that had meant that Jack had more time to spend with Peggy and the kids. But most of all he'd miss the long conversations with Barney. He was the only one who really understood his feelings about being in the army but not in the war, because he'd been in the same boat. To Jack, that had been worth the extra cost of employing Barney, and anyway the money from Aunt Laura had helped to ease the financial problems.

"I don't know how you run your place, Uncle Walter, and if you say you can't afford an extra hand then I'm sure you're right. Don't go making no assumptions about Rickyard, though. I've got that running very efficiently, thank you, and Barney was more than paying for his keep."

Walter cackled.

"You'm really are a one, Jack. Do you'm think the folks around here don't know nothing? There'm be more'n a dozen farmers in Ambridge who could tell you your running costs down to the last blade of grass on your meadow. You ain't a-been making money these past few months and more, even if you'm think it."

Jack felt the anger rising but he knew there was no point in arguing with Walter Gabriel. There wasn't even any point in being rude to him – he was totally impervious to insults.

"You and all the others can think what you want, Walter Gabriel, I don't care. I'm quite happy to go on minding my own business."

Walter cackled again and Jack was conscious that others in the bar were listening to what was being said. That didn't worry Walter.

"Don't go getting all sensitive, young feller-me-lad. I'm not out to interfere. I was only trying to offer a bit of helpful advice like the good godfather I am."

Jack groaned. He was about to be reminded for the umpteenth time that Walter had been his father's best man, and that he and his Annie had been asked to be godparents to Dan's firstborn when he was christened. Mind you, to be fair to the Gabriels, they had taken their responsibilities seriously and Jack recalled that none of his birthdays had lacked that special present from them. He just wished Walter wouldn't keep going on about it; it made him feel as if he was still a teenager.

"You might not have noticed, Uncle Walter, but I am out of short pants now. I'm a married man with two kids and I'm quite capable of taking on my own responsibilities. I don't need advice."

Walter shook his head sadly.

"That's where you'm wrong, my lad. We'm all need advice and it's the clever ones what takes it."

Jack, realising another tale of homespun wisdom was about to emerge, tried to stem the flow by ordering Walter another pint, but no sooner had Sam Crowcroft put the beer in front of them than Walter was off again.

"Even your dad – one of the best farmers in the whole of Borsetshire – isn't above taking advice even from the likes of me. There's many a time when we were young farmers struggling together that he a-listened to what I had to say, and he'd be the first to tell you that once or twice he might well have gone under if it hadn't been for the help he got from me and my Annie."

Jack took a long drink from his pint pot and settled down to listen.

"I remember one year Dan had trouble drilling his corn and could have lost his entire crop if it hadn't been for my Annie and me. His drilling machine had lost a wheel and when he put it back on he damaged the spike barrel without realising it. As soon as the horse started to pull it again, one of the spikes flew off and slashed its hind leg. The poor beast was so badly hurt, Dan had to have it put down. He tried all round the area to borrow a horse, but nobody could help because they were all doing their own drilling."

Jack had heard the story several times before but there was nothing that would have stopped Walter, now he'd started.

"I met him in this very bar when he was just about at the end of his tether, poor lad. We soon concocted a way of solving the problem. I'm a bit of a dab hand at cobbling things together, as you know, so I had a go at converting the horse's harness to fit Dan and me. It worked, and we pulled the drilling machine ourselves. It saved the day. In fact, if it hadn't been for that there might not be a Brookfield at all today!"

Walter had missed out one or two elements in the story, including the fact that his long-suffering Annie had also acted as one of the human horses, but Jack knew from Dan's account how grateful he'd been for the way Walter had stepped into the breach. He and Walter had been close friends ever since.

"But with all the new machinery around, no one's likely to have to face that sort of problem today. Have you seen this new Land Rover jeep thing that's just come onto the market?"

Walter shook his head. Mechanisation wasn't one of his strong points.

"What the heck's a Land Rover?"

"Well, it's a new all-purpose truck that's meant to replace the Jeep now that most of the Yanks have gone home and taken all their spare parts with them. It's made by Rover . . ."

"The people what make them posh cars?"

"Yes. Joe Dunnington's got a demonstration model in his garage and I had a look at it earlier today. It's fantastic. It can go anywhere, on the tracks or over the fields, and never gets stuck in the mud. Joe says it can do anything. It'll pull things as well as any tractor or you can use it as an ordinary van or car. It's made from that aluminium stuff they used in the war and it doesn't rust. Joe says it'll take a tremendous pounding without going wrong."

Jack knew that the squire was planning to buy one, and young Phil was desperately trying to persuade Mr Fairbrother that it would be a good investment. According to Joe, Jess Allard had also been very impressed with it, but there were no other local farmers ready or willing to afford one. If Jack bought one, which he was seriously thinking about, he would be joining the elite.

Walter was sceptical.

"It must be a pretty special truck but it sounds a bit much for a smallholder like you, doesn't it? You're not thinking of buying one, are you?"

Jack was annoyed by Walter's insinuation.

"Why shouldn't I be thinking about buying one? Being a smallholder doesn't mean we have to live in the Dark Ages, you know. Some of us have got progressive ideas."

Walter shook his head almost wearily.

"Your problem, young Jack, is that you'm got ideas way above your station. You be trying to compete in the wrong league. Why can't you accept your role in life? You'd be ever so much happier if you did."

"What do you mean? I'm perfectly happy!"

It was Walter's turn to buy the drinks and he ordered two pints before going on.

"No, young Jack, you're not a happy lad. You can't fool me. I can tell the frustration and bitterness that eats at your soul . . . and it's all because you won't accept things as they are . . ."

"But . . ."

"There's no use protesting, Jack. You hear me out and then you can have your say."

Jack shrugged his shoulders in resignation.

"Go on then."

"The most important thing about surviving in a small community like Ambridge is knowing your place. It's no use you swaggering about, trying to make out you're doing as well as the squire or any of the big farmers. Everybody knows you're not . . . including you. And there's no point in you trying to compete with your dad. However well you do with Rickyard, it'll never be a match for somewhere like Brookfield. You've got to be patient. If you could accept that for now you're just a smallholder and concentrate on making it profitable, then maybe some day you'll be able to afford a proper farm of your own."

"Oh, you've got me all wrong, Uncle Walter. Of course I want to make Rickyard pay . . . but it's not to compete with Dad or to save up enough money to buy a farm. I don't want to be a farmer. If I ever get enough cash in the bank, it'll be a little pub that I'll be looking for."

Jack had said the first thing that had come into his head. Walter's assessment of him had been painfully shrewd but he didn't want to admit it, even to himself – let alone to Walter Gabriel. He did want to be a farmer . . . desperately. He also wanted to be as good as his dad and he wanted people to respect him in the way they did Dan Archer. But, sadly, he was beginning to realise he just didn't have the kind of commitment and courage it took to make a good farmer. And he found it hard to bear being a nobody in a community where both his father and younger brother were highly respected by the other farmers. Maybe the idea of taking on a country pub wasn't such a bad idea? Maybe, too, he should take Walter's advice and not keep trying to fight against the odds.

Walter could see that he'd touched a raw nerve and decided to change the subject.

"It's hard to believe it's young Philip's twenty-first next week, isn't it? It seems like only weeks ago he was in short trousers. Do you think he might announce his engagement to Grace at the party?"

Jack had forgotten the party. The invitation had been lying on the mantelpiece at Rickyard Cottage for over a fortnight but he and Peggy hadn't discussed it. He had no idea whether Phil was thinking of announcing his engagement . . . although it sounded just the sort of thing he would do to make sure that he was well and truly in the limelight.

Relations between Jack and his parents had been even more strained since Barney Lee had arrived in Ambridge and Jack had turned to him more and more for advice rather than Dan. Over the past four months he'd deliberately steered clear of his family and he'd also tried to discourage Peggy from running over to Doris at Brookfield every time she wanted some sort of help with the children or the house.

It partly was because he was determined to show his independence. Although he had only a hazy recollection of what had happened out in the fields on the day of the flood, he still felt humiliated by the memory of the way Dan had just stepped in to take control. That would never happen again. There again, there was no doubt the £1,000 had made a difference. Although Doris was pleased as Punch that Jack was being helped to stand on his own feet, naturally she'd been quite upset that her other two children had been left out of Laura's generosity, and couldn't help saying so. One way or another, things had been a bit difficult and Jack had put off thinking about Phil's birthday celebrations.

"Are you going to the party, Uncle Walter?"

"Wild horses wouldn't keep me away. It sounds as if it's going to be quite a humdinger of a do. Doris always puts on a swell party, but I gather this one's going to be extra special because the Fairbrothers are going to be there. Dan's laying in enough ale to quench an army's thirst."

Jack felt slightly jealous. He remembered his own twenty-first birthday six years earlier. It had been a pretty miserable occasion because he couldn't wangle a leave pass and had been forced to spend the evening in the Naafi at Aldershot. Feeling sorry for himself, he'd got so drunk that Peggy had gone off and left him. It had been Barney and a couple of other mates who'd eventually poured him into his bed in the early hours of the morning.

That was the week before Christmas, and he and Peggy had made it up in plenty of time to have a lovely Christmas. They'd gone up to London to meet her parents and it was after a happy Christmas dinner with as many of the traditional trimmings as could be managed on wartime rationing that he'd plucked up the courage to ask Peggy to marry him.

He twisted the signet ring on his finger. That had been Peg's wedding present to him. She was a smashing girl and she'd turned out to be a perfect wife. He really admired the way she'd settled into Ambridge and was now accepted by all the village women as one of themselves. He didn't know whether or not she missed all the hustle and bustle and excitement of city life because she'd never once complained about it, even when he'd refused to take her back on a short visit. He knew he'd given her a pretty rough time on occasions, but she had terrific spirit and always bounced back. She somehow managed to keep him going even when his spirits were at their lowest . . . which, unfortunately, had been all too often.

Jack looked at the clock behind the bar. It was half-past eight. He decided to go home. It was the first time in years that he had left a pub before closing time.

"Good night, Uncle Walter. Thanks for the chat."

Walter looked at the clock and then anxiously at Jack.

"Aw heck, Jack lad, don't be like that. You'm don't have to go off in a huff. I didn't mean to bend your ear so much that it'd drive you away from your pint. Here, let me get you another one and I promise to stay as silent as the grave."

It was Jack's turn to laugh.

"Don't you worry none, Uncle Walter. It's not your conversation that's driving me away . . . but I'm going back home. To talk to my Peggy. I think it's time I gave her a bit more consideration."

He left the pub with Walter's great cackles of glee ringing in his ears and the few other men glancing surreptitiously at the clock.

When he got home to Rickyard Cottage, he found Peggy in tears. She jumped guiltily when he walked in and hurriedly tried to pretend she'd been having a sneezing fit.

"Gosh, Jack, you're home early. Is there something the matter?"

"No, there's nothing wrong. I just decided to have an early night so that I could come home and put my feet up with my wife. There's nothing wrong with that, is there?"

Peggy sniffed.

"Of course not. I'm delighted to see you."

"So what's up with you then? Why are you crying?"

She wiped her reddened eyes.

"Oh, it's nothing, Jack. I'm just feeling a bit under the weather."

"Come on, lass. This is your husband you're talking to. I know you better than that. You don't weep buckets just because you're not feeling too well. What's the problem, love?"

"I don't know that there is a problem, Jack. It's just . . . oh I don't know what it is."

"Is it because of Barney going? Are you going to miss him?"

During his six months with them, Barney had been very attentive to Peggy, making himself responsible for all sorts of chores around the house and playing regularly with the kids. Jack knew that despite her earlier reservations about having him as a guest, she'd become quite fond of him.

Peggy nodded her head.

"I suppose it's about Barney in a way . . . but not in the way you're thinking. Personally I'm delighted he's gone because now we can have the house to ourselves and be a proper family again. I mean, Barney was a lovely man but he was never one of us. I could never feel really comfortable when he was around . . . I could never slop around in my dressing gown and slippers or anything like that. At the same time, I'm very sorry he's gone because I'm worried about what it'll do to you!"

"How do you mean?"

"Well, he was a obviously a great help to you and with him being such a good pal you've tended to rely on him a lot over the few months he's been here. You're bound to miss him and I don't want to see you moping around the place like a bear with a sore head."

Jack took her gently in his arms and looked at her reddened eyes.

"Oh, Peggy. You don't have very much faith in me, do you?"

"That's not true . . ."

"Shush, lass, don't say anything. I haven't given you much cause to respect me, but I've a feeling I'm going to turn over a new leaf and Barney's going is just the kick up the pants I need. I was with Uncle Walter in the pub tonight and he gave me a real dressing down about what a dope I've been in trying to be what I'm not and trying to compete with Dad."

Peggy smiled. Having heard more than a few of Walter's monologues herself, she was no longer surprised that Jack had come home early. He was a refugee from homespun philosophy.

"No, don't laugh, Peg. The old boy was right. I have been making a pig's ear of things. It's time that you and I found our place in Ambridge. We're not up there with the big farmers. We're just ordinary folk . . . smallholders trying to scratch an honest living and there's nothing wrong in that. We'll have a go at being good at what we've set out to do and if that doesn't work we'll try our hand at something else."

Peggy was delighted. She'd been beginning to feel she couldn't keep up with Jack's helter-skelter existence and she'd watched in despair as most of Aunt Laura's money had disappeared on machinery and equipment that was totally unnecessary on their nine acres.

"Does that mean you won't be spending money on one of those new Land Rovers?"

"Aye, Peg. It means precisely that. There'll be no more highfalutin ideas around Rickyard. We'll forget about the great chrysanthemum scheme, at least for the time being, and we can also get shot of some of the other fancy gear we've got around the place. We'll use the cash to make life a bit better for you and the kids."

Peggy had been worrying herself sick about the extra costs she was going to have to face in a couple of months' time when Jennifer started at school. Now she could stop worrying. She smiled and hugged Jack.

"Why is it that one kind word from you, Jack Archer, and my knees seem to melt? I do love you."

Over her shoulder, Jack noticed the birthday invitation on the mantelpiece. He untangled himself and picked it up.

"We haven't talked about this, Peg. Will we be going?"

Peggy fingered the gold-edged card wistfully.

"It's up to you, Jack."

"No it's not, lass. There are two of us in this together. It's up to *us* whether or not we go. What do you think?"

"But how can we go? Neither of us has been at Brookfield for ages and I thought you didn't want to have anything to do with the family. We can't suddenly change our minds and just waltz up because they're having a fancy party. What on earth would Mum and Dad think?"

Jack thought for a moment. Was Peggy right? No, she wasn't.

"I know exactly what will happen if we say we'd like to go. Mum will burst into tears and Dad will try not to look too pleased. They're family, Peg. They'll understand about the last few months."

"Oh, Jack, are you sure? I'd love to go. I can't remember the last time I went to a party, and you won't believe this, but I've never been to a twenty-first in my life."

"Don't remind me, Peg. I was just thinking what it was like when we were both twenty-one. Neither of us exactly got the key-of-the-door treatment, did we?"

Peggy laughed.

"The only key you were likely to see was the one to the cells at Aldershot. You got as drunk as a skunk and they threw you out of the Naafi!"

"I don't remember that."

"I'm not surprised. The state you were in, it would be a miracle if you remembered anything. I've never told you this before, but that night you actually told *my* sergeant major to go and take a running jump at herself! You were lucky she didn't put you in the guardroom and throw away the key of the door! It was only because I was able to charm her that you got away with it."

"You must have used some charm, Peg. She was a right old dragon."

Jack picked up the invitation to Philip's party again.

"So that's agreed then? We say we'll be delighted to attend?"

"Yes, Jack, that'll be wonderful."

She thought for a minute and then looked at the clock. It was still only nine o'clock.

"Why don't you nip across to Brookfield now . . . and maybe have a drink with Dad while you're there?"

Jack pulled his shoulders back.

"I think that's a good idea, Peg. It'll be nice to walk up the drive just as a member of the family paying a visit instead of skulking around trying to work out how much better Dad's doing than me. That really is independence."

CHAPTER TWELVE

Great roars of laughter rolled around the village hall, but the speaker on the small stage was totally unperturbed. He'd got used to farmers' reactions when he came to talk to them about the need to listen to the farming information being put out on the wireless by the Ministry of Agriculture and outlined his latest plan to make the propaganda more palatable.

Godfrey Baseley, the BBC's agricultural officer for the Midlands, had been talking to NFU groups in the region for some time, trying to encourage more farmers to tune in to the programmes and soliciting ideas for making them more interesting. It had been at such a meeting that one farmer had suggested that what was needed was more of "a Dick Barton approach". This a-thrill-a-minute daily serial was one of the most popular programmes on the wireless. Its signature tune, "The Devil's Gallop", was the signal for millions of listeners to grip the arms of their chairs while they caught up with the latest exploits of Dick and his two faithful assistants, Jock Anderson and Snowy White.

When he'd first heard the idea, Godfrey Baseley had laughed as loudly as anybody. The thought of dramatising a farmer's problems with warble fly or a Ministry information sheet about weed control was almost too ludicrous for words. However, the idea wouldn't go away and the more it churned through his head, the less ridiculous it became. The December meeting of the Ambridge and District NFU was the third at which he'd introduced the idea, and the laughter that greeted it echoed the response he'd had everywhere else.

His talk over, he took the chance at the end of the meeting to chat to one or two members over a glass of beer and some sandwiches. Jack Archer was there, representing the Ambridge smallholders on the committee. Godfrey asked him if he ever listened to the farming programmes.

"To tell you the truth, Mr Baseley, I hardly ever bother. They either tell me things I already know or they're so complicated that I can't understand them. My wife Peggy is a great listener, though, and if she hears anything useful she passes it on to me."

"What do you really think of the idea of putting the programme into the form of a play?"

Jack laughed.

"If you're talking about the Dick Barton idea, I think it's daft. You'd never get anyone excited about agricultural life. You know as well as anyone that our life is very routine. We just follow the seasons year after year. Not much ever changes. You'd bore the listeners to death."

Godfrey Baseley shrugged his shoulders and nodded. There was no point in pursuing the thought any further. He'd have to find another way of livening up his programmes.

When Jack got home from the meeting, he mentioned the suggestion to Peggy and she, too, found it very funny. She was an avid fan of Dick Barton and just couldn't see the programme's fast-moving style being adapted to farming topics.

"If you were talking about the adventures of Dick Barton, though, Jack, it must've been a bit more interesting than most NFU meetings."

"Aye, it was. Apart from that daft idea, Baseley's a very stimulating character and I'm sure he's set most of us thinking about what we've got to do to get the industry on its feet. He says it's no use leaving it to other people to get things moving. He's right, of course; we've all got to get off our backsides and work harder."

Peggy was delighted to hear Jack talk so positively. In the months since Barney Lee had gone back to Cornwall, he really had turned over a new leaf, not only working full-out on the smallholding, but also finding more time to spend with her and the kids. Quite often now, instead of putting his feet up with the paper, he'd take them off for a long run in the car on Sundays and they'd have the kind of picnics she'd enjoyed so much when they were house-hunting. He always made sure he had at least a few minutes to play with the children before they went to bed, and sometimes he'd go as far as reading them stories in bed.

He'd also encouraged Peggy to set up a small poultry business, helping her to get it started until he could see it was running smoothly, when he'd left her to get on with it. Now she was doing quite well selling eggs to the village shop and one or two other local customers. Peggy had begun to enjoy life in the countryside. Jack had at long last dug over a nice big patch of ground close to the house and she'd been able to establish a very good vegetable garden. It was now as she had imagined it many years earlier when Jack had first offered her the chance to escape from London and its sweatshops and traffic and noise. She knew it wasn't a roses-round-the-door paradise, but she loved the fresh air and the quiet.

As far as she knew, Jack had given up gambling, and he had certainly cut down on his drinking. He was still a regular at The Bull, but she believed him when he said he spent more time playing darts than downing beer. He hadn't been late home since Barney Lee had gone back to Cornwall, and although he'd been quite merry on two or three occasions, she hadn't seen him drunk since then either.

What pleased her most, however, was that they were back on good terms with his family. She had been really upset at not being able to pop across to Brookfield whenever she felt like it and she'd missed the long chats with Doris.

The turning point had been Philip's twenty-first birthday party. Jack had been absolutely right about his mum and dad's reactions. When he'd first gone back to see them to say they'd like to go to the party, Doris had cried and Dan had shaken him warmly by the hand, and within minutes all the past strain and stress had disappeared.

On the night of the party, Peggy had one of the greatest surprises of her life . . . her mother had turned up for it!

Jack had made all the arrangements. His parents had readily agreed that Mrs P could stay at Brookfield for a few days, and then he'd driven down to London, picked his mother-in-law up in the car and brought her back to Ambridge without Peggy knowing anything about it. It was a wonderful moment when she'd made her appearance at the party, and Peggy wasn't sure who had cried the most . . . she or her mum or Doris!

"Aren't you listening to me, Peg?"

"Sorry, Jack. I was miles away. I was just thinking about the party at Brookfield when you suddenly produced Mum as a surprise for me."

"That's funny, because that's what I was trying to talk to you about. I was wondering whether you wanted to invite your mum and dad up for Christmas or if you'd like to go down to London for a change?"

Although Peggy hadn't been back to London in nearly five years and she still missed her parents quite often, she never missed London itself. Most of her friends had married and moved away and she'd lost touch with them.

"I don't think Mum could cope with you and me and the kids, Jack, but it's a lovely thought. Dad would be thrilled to see us. He still hasn't seen either of the kids, you know."

Her father's health had continued to deteriorate and he'd never been able to join his wife on her occasional visits to Ambridge.

"I tell you what, Peg. Why don't we ask Mum to look after the kids for a couple of days? And I'll get one of the Allard lads to keep an eye on the stock. Then we'll drive to London, do a bit of shopping and maybe go to a show in the evening. We can end up at your place and bring your mum and dad back here in the car. What do you think of that as an idea?"

Peggy was overwhelmed.

"Jack, that would be terrific."

She was going to ask if they could afford it and if Jack really could organise help and so on, but she decided against it. She just accepted the offer.

Jack kept his word and three days before Christmas they drove down to London. All was well until they hit the city, and that's when Jack got lost. He wasn't used to the traffic which was even worse than usual as the crowds of Christmas shoppers added to the normal congestion. Jack's temper wasn't at its best by the time they eventually found somewhere to park just off Oxford Circus. There was only an hour or two left for shopping but it was probably just as well because squeezing through the crowds was also beginning to test Jack's patience.

They tried to have tea in Lyons' Corner House but it was packed solid and they had to make do with cakes and sandwiches in a small café in Piccadilly after Jack had refused point blank to go into Fortnum and Masons.

The journey back to Ambridge had its difficult moments, too. Peggy's father insisted on stopping at almost every public lavatory on the 140-mile route and every time the speedometer went above 50 miles an hour, Mrs P let out a squeal of panic and forced Jack to slow down.

Once home, however, all was well. Albert Perkins settled himself in a comfortable chair where he could look out of the window, watch Jack at work in the fields and listen to the wireless at the same time. He had all his meals served there and Mrs P said he'd never seemed happier. For her part, she buzzed around the village saying hello to all her old friends and going for walks with both the children.

Peggy had to work like a slave to keep everyone fed and comfortable, but she was in her element. She had learned her lessons from Doris Archer and she was beginning to feel that she was slowly but surely becoming almost as much of a farmer's wife herself.

Jack watched it all with a kind of benign resignation. He didn't really feel part of things, but he was happy that it was his efforts that had contrived to make it all possible, and that brought its own contentment and reward. He felt he was head of his own family, after having lived in the shadows of his parents for so long.

Peggy could sense his quiet satisfaction.

"Happy, Jack?"

"I'm very happy now, lass."

Christmas went past in a flash of eating, drinking and general merriment and the farming community started getting ready for Plough Monday and the start of another agricultural year . . . but before that, there was another round of celebrations for the New Year.

For more years than most folk could remember, the tenant of Brookfield Farm had played host on New Year's Eve to as many neighbours as could crowd into the place. Nobody knew why Brookfield was the chosen place but Dan's father had acquired the responsibility somewhere around the turn of the century. When Dan took on the tenancy a few days after his twenty-first birthday in 1917, he and his mother had cheerfully accepted what others might have seen as a chore. When he married Doris, she had said she'd leave him if he didn't let her continue the tradition!

This year was Doris's twenty-ninth New Year's Eve party at Brookfield, but she planned it as carefully as she had the first one when she was still a blushing bride, only fourteen days after her wedding in 1921. Peggy felt especially privileged that she was allowed to help her, for Doris jealously guarded her rights as a hostess, and the kitchen at Rickyard was pressed into service from Boxing Day onwards, preparing the cooked meats that would be needed to feed the hungry hordes.

Peggy's parents had been invited to stay on, but Mr Perkins was determined to be back in London to see in the New Year. He had a feeling it might be his last, he said, and if that was the case he wanted to spend it in his own home with all his old pals around him.

"No offence to you and your people, Jack, you understand."

Jack did understand and, although he could ill afford the time, he drove them back to London the day after Boxing Day. All the way back in the car, Mrs P said how much she liked Ambridge and especially the people.

"I did so enjoy talking to them all. They're ever so friendly and they don't seem to pry as much as my neighbours do in London. I think my favourite people are the Gabriels. Annie is a lovely woman and that husband of hers is a real charmer."

Jack almost crashed the car in surprise. Of all the words he'd ever heard applied to Walter, charming had never been one of them. He must be a bit of a dark horse with the ladies if he'd managed to impress the redoubtable Mrs P.

When she was sure her husband had dozed off in the back seat, Mrs P changed the topic and, to Jack's discomfort, started on much more personal matters.

"I hope you don't mind me asking, Jack, but how are you and my Peg getting on these days?"

"We're getting on fine, thank you."

"Are you sure?"

"Yes, I'm sure. Why do you ask?"

Jack kept his eyes fixed on the road ahead but he could tell Mrs P was staring at him intently.

"Well, I ask because I know my Peg. She's a very cheerful girl at heart and there have been times not so long ago when I could tell that she wasn't all that happy. You and she haven't been having any rows, have you?"

"No, not recently. Peg and me have had our ups and downs like any married couple, but it's never been anything serious."

He could feel her eyes on him.

"Have you stopped drinking then?"

The questions were becoming increasingly uncomfortable.

"What do you mean, Mrs P? What's Peggy been saying?"

"You know quite well what I mean, Jack Archer. And I haven't heard a word of it from Peg. I don't need to. I pick up a lot of gossip when I'm in Ambridge and there are one or two things I've heard that don't please me as a mother-in-law, and one of them has been your heavy drinking."

Jack was relieved that at least it wasn't Peggy who'd been talking behind his back.

"I was drinking a bit too much when I got out of the army. I found it very difficult to settle down again in civvy street, but that's all behind me now. I have a regular pint or two at The Bull, but nothing more than that. Has somebody being saying different?"

Mrs P didn't answer. She just grunted noncommittally.

"I was none too happy to hear about your . . . er . . . relationship with the schoolteacher girl . . . what's her name . . . Elsie Catcher."

Jack almost stopped the car. He hadn't even clapped eyes on Elsie since the Royal Wedding celebrations and that must have been at least a couple of years back. He knew Barney Lee had been out with Elsie once or twice and she may have been back at Rickyard Cottage with him on some occasion, but certainly not while Jack was around.

"I haven't got any relationship with Elsie Catcher, other than that she's been living around Ambridge for a long time and we've therefore been kind of friendly in the usual way. You couldn't possibly have heard anything different to that. Nobody's daft enough to spread rumours about me and her."

"So it's not true that you stepped out with her before you went into the army and wrote to her while you were away?"

Jack had forgotten all about that. He must have been about sixteen or seventeen at the time. He was now beginning to feel quite cross.

"Look Mrs P, I'm not very keen on this inquisition. Elsie and I did go out for a while when we were teenagers and maybe I did write to her for a while when I was in the army, but what's the harm in that? If you're suggesting that I've been playing around behind Peggy's back, that's a pretty nasty thing to say."

"I'm not saying anything of the kind. I was only asking straightforward questions."

"Straightforward, my eye! They're all innuendo and I don't like it. I know you don't approve of me. I know you think your daughter's married beneath herself. Well, you're entitled to your view, Mrs P. But for better or worse, Peg is married to me and it's about time you accepted it. I love Peg and my kids, and there's nothing I would do to hurt them."

Mrs P adjusted her hat with the silly black feathers.

"I'm very glad to hear it, Jack. I'm sorry if you should think I don't like you. That's not true either. It wouldn't be natural if a mother wasn't worried about her daughter marrying a strange man and then disappearing into the back of beyond, now would it?"

"No, I suppose not."

"Well, maybe this little conversation will have cleared the air between us."

Jack hadn't realised that the air had to be cleared, but at least he was glad that Mrs P had stopped rabbiting on.

The journey back to Ambridge was wonderfully peaceful. Once he almost stopped to pick up a hitch-hiker, but decided against it, when he thought that whoever it was might have talked as much as Mrs P. He remembered getting caught like that once before when he had stopped to give one of the village women a lift into Ambridge on his way back from Borchester. She was Emily Spenlow, a dotty old dear who believed in spiritualism, and all the way back she'd insisted on

163

telling Jack about how she was in constant touch with her husband who had died several years earlier, and how he was always giving her messages about things that were going to happen.

By a strange coincidence, she said, she'd been talking to her husband about Jack only the day before, and she was full of interesting things about his future. Jack didn't believe for one moment in her psychic powers, but he listened with amusement when she informed him that he would come into money one day and own quite a big property. It wouldn't be a farmhouse, she said. More like a restaurant or an inn. With a grin, Jack had recalled his own fleeting thoughts about taking on a pub tenancy, but had quickly declined Mrs Spenlow's offer of a cup of tea when they arrived at her house.

On the day of the New Year's Eve party, Jack had ferried over all the food Peggy had prepared from Rickyard Cottage to Brookfield in his car – getting his wrists slapped by both Peggy and his mother when he tried to have a quick nibble from the mouth-watering hams and the legs of lamb – and had finally gone back to fetch Peggy and two very excited little girls. They were going to sleep at Brookfield for the night, a treat they always enjoyed because everyone still made a great fuss of them. Even Philip had been known to tell them bedtime stories.

Once the guests started arriving, Jack found himself stationed in the little scullery off the kitchen where he drew the pints from the great barrel of beer, while Phil dashed around handing them out. It dawned on Jack that his younger brother was being unusually helpful. At his own birthday party earlier in the year he'd spent most of the evening in a corner with his girlfriend.

"Where's Grace tonight, Phil?"

"Grace who?"

Jack guessed that there'd been a row between the two.

"Grace Fairbrother . . . you know, the girl you were going to marry the last time we talked!"

His young brother frowned.

"Oh, that Grace. She's not around any more. I've got a new girl, but unfortunately she couldn't make it tonight. She's still down in the West Country where she's been spending the Christmas break with her family."

Jack would probably have left it at that, but his brother looked very unhappy.

"Come on, Phil lad, tell your big brother your problems."

Philip hesitated and then looked around to see that there was no one else within earshot. The kitchen was empty.

"I am in a mess, Jack. I've made a right botch of it with Grace. She caught me flirting with one of the girls in the estate office and she created an awful fuss. Stupidly, I told her to get lost and then I dated the other girl out of spite. Since she found out she won't even speak to me. What can I do?"

Jack smiled. It was a relief to learn that there was something his younger brother wasn't particularly good at, but he could see the lad was suffering and he felt sorry for him. He gave him the benefit of his advice as an older man of the world.

"There's not too much you can do, Phil. Women are very contrary creatures and if you push too hard to talk to Grace, that's the last thing on earth she'll let happen. If I were you, I'd try to play it very calmly and pretend it doesn't matter whether she ever talks to you or not. She'll soon come round."

"Are you sure?"

"No, lad, I'm not sure. You can never be sure where women are concerned . . . but take my advice, give the casual approach a try. You've got nothing to lose!"

A bellow for more beer came from the next room and Phil rushed off with hurried thanks for the advice. Jack doubted whether he'd actually take it.

Almost as Philip went out the door, young Christine came in looking flushed and angry.

"Ah, Jack, I've been looking for you. I need your protection."

"Protection? Who on earth do you need protecting from?"

"That chap Paul Johnson. He's been pestering me for ages and he's got hands like an octopus. Can I stay and chat to you?"

He laughed and gave her a little hug.

"This really is big brother night, isn't it? I've just been handing out advice to our Phil and now it's your turn."

"Oh, but I don't want any advice. I don't need any. I just want to stay and chat somewhere out of arm's length of Paul Johnson. What's wrong with Phil? Is he still mooning over his lost love?"

"Come on now, Chris, let's not get at Phil. It'll be your turn to suffer like that next."

"Not on your life it won't! I hate men. They're boring. They can only think of one thing and they never want to talk about anything interesting."

"Interesting like what?"

Jack didn't really need to ask. Christine's obsession with horses showed no signs of abating and she was talking about trying to raise the cash to set up her own stables.

"Well, they could talk a little about horses, couldn't they? I mean everybody knows something about horses."

"How far have you got with your idea of setting up your own business?"

She looked glum.

"Precisely nowhere. I think even if I work for the Milk Marketing Board for the rest of my life, I still won't be able to raise the cash I need. It's frightfully expensive."

"What you really need is a rich young man who'll be happy to indulge you and set you up in the livery stables business."

"Oh, thanks very much, I'm sure. That's what I want like a hole in the head. I remember you once telling me how important it is to have a feeling of independence.

Well that's what I need. I don't want to be reliant on somebody else who can tell me what to do or not to do with my money."

Jack smiled at her.

"You've got a good memory, sis, and now that you remind me of my words of wisdom, all I can do is repeat them. You keep your independence if you possibly can!"

Just then Peggy put her head round the kitchen door.

"Come on you two, it's getting very close to midnight. Dad wants everyone together for the bells."

Dan had gathered everybody round the wireless in a big circle. He called for silence and a hush descended on the crowded room as the last seconds of the year died away. Jack put his arms round Peggy and as the bells rang out to mark the birth of another year, he kissed her.

"Happy New Year, Peg."

Peggy kissed him back.

"Happy New Year to you, Jack." Everyone linked hands to join in the tuneless but lusty singing of "Auld Lang Syne". At the words "auld acquaintance" Jack thought fleetingly of some of the lads he'd met in the army . . . especially the ones who'd never come back from the war and those who came back so badly wounded that they'd never lead normal lives. He pushed the painful memories away quickly and thought instead of Barney Lee down in Cornwall. Would he ever meet him again?

As the noise subsided to a general hubbub, Jack pulled Peggy close again.

"Well, Peg, here's to a really good year for you, me and the girls."

"That's my wish too, Jack, but have you got a New Year's resolution?"

He thought for a moment and remembered his conversation with Walter Gabriel . . . about knowing his place in the community and not trying to be something he could never be.

"Yes, Peg, I have. I resolve that in the next year I'll do my best to let the folk of Ambridge get to know me . . . as plain and simple Jack Archer."

TO THE VICTOR THE SPOILS

Daniel Archer escapes the mud of Flanders to take over the tenancy of Brookfield Farm on the death of his father in 1916. It is his younger brother Ben who is most devastated by the horrors of the Great War – try as he will, he cannot forget the stench and din of Passchendaele. On his return to Ambridge at the end of the war he is unable to settle down to work on the farm, and chafes beneath Daniel's authority. To make matters worse, both brothers are interested in the same girl, Doris Forrest, daughter of the local gamekeeper . . .

To the Victor the Spoils is the first volume in *The Archers* trilogy. It is the story of young Daniel Archer's struggle to make a success of Brookfield Farm in the agricultural depression of the early twenties. And it is the story of the early friendships, the loves and rivalries that will play their part in shaping the later fortunes of the small Borsetshire village.

BORCHESTER ECHOES

Phil and Jill Archer's younger daughter Elizabeth, is using her job in the tele-sales department of the *Borchester Echo* to try and break through into the world of journalism. Always on the lookout for news stories to impress proprietor Jack Woolley, she enlists the help of her boyfriend Robin Fairbrother and of winebar-owner Nelson Gabriel to investigate what she imagines to be a swindle being conducted by a local antiques dealer.

Meanwhile her private life is carried on at a hectic pace. Robin Fairbrother offers her the entrée to the world of fast cars and good living, but she is still amused by the antics of hooray-Henry Nigel Pargetter, and cannot resist a minor fling with Terry Barford, serving with the Army in Germany, who she joins for a weekend in Berlin.

Elizabeth gets her story . . . but not quite the job on the *Borchester Echo* she anticipated.

Another BBC novel:

KING STREET JUNIOR

King Street Junior is the popular Radio 4 comedy
series about life in a multi-racial inner-city school. In
this wry and amusing novel, based on the series
which he created following his own experiences as a
supply teacher, Jim Eldridge portrays the funny side
of day-to-day school life.

Here is the chance to meet Phillip Sims, young
solicitor turned teacher and King Street Junior's
newest recruit, Mr Beeston, the harassed headmaster,
and all the other eccentric members of staff at this
lively and problem-beset junior school. With
characters such as militant Mr Long, Mrs Rudd,
transport-obsessed Mr Holliday and the long-suffering
school secretary, Mrs Stone, Jim Eldridge's novel
never fails to bring out the humour in the trials and
tribulations of teaching.

What the critics said about the radio series

'a unique balance of fun, compassion and social
conscience . . . wonderful real-life feel'
Alan Cunningham, *Mail on Sunday*

'its excellence derives from the well-judged scripts of
Jim Eldridge'
David Self, *Times Educational Supplement*

'a pithily accurate picture of what it is like to teach
large numbers of children in an ill-equipped school'
Gillian Reynolds, *Daily Telegraph*

'the humour arises naturally . . . schools being
essentially comic places anyway'
Val Arnold-Foster, *Guardian*

You may also enjoy this selection of BBC quizbooks:

TELLY ADDICTS
with a foreword by Noel Edmonds

How much do you think *you* know about television?

- Who is Cagney and Lacey's boss?
- How many husbands called Tanner did Elsie Tanner have?
- Who are the presenters of *The Clothes Show*?
- Which dolphin had its own series?

Set yourself to answer these and hundreds more questions from Noel Edmonds' popular television quiz show, and find out if you can really call yourself a Telly Addict!

Lots of chances to probe the mysteries of Noel's Prop Bag too!

MASTERTEAM
with a foreword by Angela Rippon

Can you face up to the quick-fire questions of *Masterteam*, BBC's fast-moving team-challenge quiz show hosted by Angela Rippon?

- Who wrote the futuristic novel *1985*?
- Who is the patron saint of policemen, paratroopers and grocers?
- What was the name of the snail in *The Magic Roundabout*?
- What was the first single released by the Beatles on the Apple label?

With hundreds of questions on literature, pop and classical music, history, geography, cinema, sport, food and drink, the living world, there's something here for all the family to answer!

BRAIN OF SPORT

Prove yourself a sporting champion by answering these questions from Radio 2's popular and long-running quiz show *Brain of Sport*.

- Who took 15 wickets in a test match during the 1985–6 season?
- What does the D in Arnold D Palmer stand for?
- Who was the first Briton in 1981 to win the world long track Speedway Championship?
- Which Football League Club played its home matches at Peele Croft?

With hundreds of questions on all the most popular sports – soccer, rugby, cricket, tennis, athletics, snooker, swimming, and horse racing – this BBC quizbook will really test your knowledge of the record books!

FIRST CLASS
with a foreword by Debbie Greenwood

- Which woollen hat sounds like a fruit?
- What is Prince's full name?
- Subtract the year of Magna Carta from the year of Magna Carta from the year of the battle of Waterloo, and what number are you left with?
- What would you do with a Sopwith Camel?

First Class, BBC 1's popular, fast-moving quiz hosted by Debbie Greenwood, is now on the screen on Saturday evenings.

Have fun answering hundreds of questions from the show – on general knowledge, pop music, the movies, sport, and news of the '80s.

Whether you're aged eight or eighty, you're bound to find something here to test your wits and ingenuity!

A QUESTION OF SPORT

The book of BBC tv's leading quiz game.

•

Pit your sporting wits against the top national and international stars.

•

Put yourself in Bill Beaumont's or Emlyn Hughes's team and see how well you can answer *A Question of Sport*'s testing rounds, including the Pictureboard round, Home and Away, the One-Minute round, and Mystery Personality.

•

Featuring sporting profiles of Emlyn's and Bill's guests – popular personalities like Bryan Robson, Hana Mandlikova, Mike Gatting, Daley Thompson, Clive Allen and American Football's Walter Payton.

•

Hundreds of questions on sports ranging from athletics to archery and soccer to skiing.

•

Pre-match advice from Captains Bill Beaumont and Emlyn Hughes.

•

More than 150 full-colour and black and white photographs.